Murder in Stonehill Manor
A Samantha Degan Mystery

by

Jane O'Brien

For information, email **Cozy Cat Press**, cozycatpress@aol.com or visit our website at: www.cozycatpress.com

COZY CAT
P R E S S

ISBN: 978-1-946063-16-8

Printed in the United States of America

Cover design by Paula Ellenberger
www.paulaellenberger.com

1 2 3 4 5 6 7 8 9 10

A heartfelt thank you to all of those who have helped me with my writing—those who encouraged me from the start, those who have read and edited my works and those who have praised my writing and enjoy reading about good, clean murder.

PROLOGUE

Samantha Degan nervously watched the clock as she sat at her desk on the second floor of the west wing of the stately mansion known as Stonehill Manor. It was almost seven o'clock in the morning and the house was eerily quiet. Her employer, Fenwick Stonehill, was normally awake and calling for her long before this.

The phone on her desk buzzed.

"Samantha, this is Judy Pryor, Professor Stonehill's night nurse. I'm afraid I was called away last night and wasn't able to finish my shift. One of my children was running a fever and my older daughter was frightened. The Professor said he would be all right on his own until his day nurse arrived at eight o'clock."

"Judy, you know Professor Stonehill cannot be left alone. You should have called me or George before you left."

"I don't expect you to understand. You don't have children. You don't know how difficult it is to leave them alone all night."

"Thank you for calling." Samantha was trying to keep her voice calm, "I'll check on Professor Stonehill right away."

Samantha thought of paging George but knew he'd be in the stables tending to the horses as he did every morning. She decided to check Professor Stonehill on her own.

She ran up the stairs to the third floor. There was an elevator but it was slow, and she didn't want to waste any time getting to her boss. Fenwick Stonehill's mind was still as sharp as ever at eighty-one; however, his body had begun deteriorating fifteen years ago. He could walk only very short distances and getting out of bed without help was excruciatingly painful for him.

Samantha raced down the long hallway to her boss's suite of rooms. She knocked on the door.

"Professor Stonehill, may I come in?"

When there was no answer, she pushed the door open and walked into the darkened room. The heavy curtains hadn't been opened, and there were only streaks of sunlight coming through spaces between the heavy draperies.

The Professor was in his wheelchair behind his desk with his head bent forward. Samantha thought he was asleep. She walked toward him, calling his name softly. That was when she noticed a small streak of sunlight from the window reflecting on a shiny object protruding from Professor Stonehill's back.

It didn't register at first, but suddenly Samantha recognized it as the sterling silver letter opener that she used every morning to open the mail. Now it was embedded in her employer's back. Without thinking or worrying about the pain he was in, she reached over and pulled the object out. The Professor's shirt was covered with blood stains. She heard a scream and the crashing of dishes as Gretchen Carlson, the kitchen aide, walked into the room carrying Professor Stonehill's breakfast.

Gretchen turned and ran down the hallway on her plump little legs, screaming all the way "She killed him! She killed him!"

*****

Still holding the letter opener, Samantha took Professor Stonehill's hand. It felt cold and lifeless, but she refused to believe he was dead. She reached for the phone with her left hand and dialed 911. Her right hand still clenched the opener's silver handle and she couldn't let it go.

George Blake came rushing through the door. He approached Samantha and carefully took the letter opener out of her hand.

"What happened here, Samantha?" he asked.

"Professor Stonehill had the letter opener in his back," she cried. "Help him, George. Please help him," Samantha said through her sobs.

Gretchen was now standing by the door crying uncontrollably and repeating, "She did it. Miss Samantha killed poor Professor Stonehill."

Upon hearing her name, Samantha looked up and saw the entire staff staring at her. From Calvin Hensley, the chauffeur, to Millie Osborne, the upstairs maid, she saw a look of horror on all their faces.

Samantha didn't know it, but she had blood on her hands when the paramedics arrived. Shortly afterward, Detectives Joseph Fletcher and Robin Wells entered the suite.

Detective Wells ushered the staff out of the room while Detective Fletcher questioned Samantha.

"The lady is in shock, Detective," said George, "can't this wait?"

"It can wait until we get her to the station. In the meantime, I want this room secured; it's now a crime scene. Our boys will be doing a thorough search of the suite. Detective Wells will interview every one on the staff."

*****

Samantha felt the cold handcuffs being placed on her wrists. She had stopped crying and now only felt overwhelming sadness as she saw Professor Stonehill's body being taken away on a gurney.

CHAPTER 1

Samantha Degan was voted the most likely to succeed in the senior class of her high school. School work came easily to her. As the youngest child of Colleen and Archie Degan, Samantha was a "happy surprise," as her mother always told her. Her youngest brother was ten-years-old when Samantha came into the world. After four boys, the Degans had given up hope of ever having a little girl.

The Degan family never had a lot of money. Archie was a supervisor in the parts department of a local factory. Colleen worked in the pharmacy of a supermarket. With five hungry mouths to feed, the family lived frugally but the children were happy and they always had food on the table and shoes on their feet.

It was a struggle but with the help of their children's part-time jobs and steadfast determination, they were able to send all five of them to college. Samantha often heard her parents talk about the cruise they planned to take after she, the last of their brood, earned her degree.

Samantha had always loved history. Her plans were to be a high school history teacher, but as time went on, she found she had a knack for writing. She began taking more writing classes and by the time she graduated, she knew writing was in her future.

Her journalism professor, Professor Hendricks, encouraged her to continue her education and earn a master's degree. Samantha was torn. She knew even with a part-time job; she would be unable to swing the cost of school and a place to live. She refused to ask her parents for more money than they'd already contributed for her education. As it happened, Professor Hendricks had studied under Professor Fenwick Stonehill several years before and knew he was looking for an assistant to help him write his memoirs. He told Samantha that the job not only came with a generous salary, it also included room and board at Stonehill Manor.

Stonehill Manor was well-known in the college town of Lancashire, England. Other than Lancashire Hospital and Lancashire University, it was the largest building in town. Lancashire had been founded in the mid-eighteen hundreds by Professor Stonehill's great-grandfather, Elton Stonehill. Elton's own father had been a successful architect and builder in Lancashire. Elton was the youngest son of the Stonehill family. His older brothers followed in their father's footsteps, designing and building homes and businesses. Elton felt he was not taken seriously by either his father or his brothers. His grandmother died, leaving him a considerable inheritance. At the age of twenty-six, he'd had enough of his family's condescending attitude. He packed his belongings and booked passage on a ship heading for America and a new life. After wandering for a few months, he discovered acres of undeveloped land in western New York. He eventually purchased the land and used his knowledge of the building industry to begin construction of New Lancashire.

He had no trouble finding willing workers to help him build his dream town. After completing six buildings, Elton discovered it was easier to build a town than it was to establish one. With no success in renting his buildings, and his inheritance dwindling, he decided to turn one of the structures into a dance hall and saloon. Soon New Lancashire was gaining a reputation, but not the kind Elton had envisioned.

He'd almost given up hope when Vito Russo, an aging traveling salesman, told him he had the perfect soil for growing grapes. As a last resort, Elton hired the old man to teach him everything he knew about planting grapevines and producing wine. Within five years, Lancashire became well-known as an up and coming addition to the wine industry. Elton closed the dance hall and began building more houses. Businesses were started and people began arriving and buying the houses. At some point—Elton was never sure when it happened—New Lancashire became known simply as Lancashire. As the town grew, so did Elton's wealth. He built Stonehill Manor on the highest hill overlooking the town on the south side and the vineyards on the north. He married the bank president's daughter, Mary Coleridge. Mary gave birth to a son, Langley. Langley knew at an early age, he wanted to help people. His father agreed he would make a fine physician. To keep his son close by, Elton built a hospital. It was only one building at the time but it served the purpose. After graduation, Langley came home to Lancashire, married his college sweetheart and raised a son, Hawthorne, Fenwick's father. In time, the vineyards and winery were sold as Elton's son and grandson had no interest in the industry. The stately Stonehill Manor and its surrounding acreage remained as the living quarters for the Stonehill family.

Samantha drove her twelve-year-old VW bug up the winding driveway to the largest house she'd ever seen. She continued driving around to the back of the mansion where she noticed a sign that read *Service Entrance*.

A huge man opened the door.

"How can I help you, miss?" he asked in a pleasant but commanding tone.

Samantha was not easily intimidated but she felt her knees begin to tremble. "Good morning, sir. My name is Samantha Degan; I've come to apply for the personal assistant opening."

"Yes, we've been expecting you. Why didn't you use the front door, Miss Degan?" the booming voice asked. "Never mind, follow me. Professor Stonehill is waiting in the library for you."

Samantha's jaw dropped as she walked through the halls of the mansion. Everywhere she looked, she saw fine fabrics, beautiful paintings, polished wood, and gorgeous carpets. The understated elegance in each room could only reflect the exquisite taste and wealth of the occupants of the manor and of old money.

The huge man told her his name was George Blake. He was an all-around handyman and acted as a protector for Professor Stonehill when he ventured out of the mansion.

She was surprised when George introduced her to Professor Stonehill. She knew he was in his eighties, but didn't expect anyone so frail. He was seated in a wheelchair close to a massive fireplace. The fire was blazing on this chilly March morning.

"Come, sit down, my dear." His voice was strong and confident. It surprised Samantha that someone whose body was obviously wearing out could speak so powerfully. His eyes sparkled as he spoke. His face was very pleasant. Samantha imagined he had been very handsome in his younger days. His hair was white—not gray like her father's—but pure white. She felt comfortable with him and the trepidation she'd felt when she'd arrived had disappeared.

Professor Stonehill began asking questions about Samantha, her ambitions and her family. He explained that the Stonehill staff had been with the family for many years.

"You met George Blake. George is my protector; he is, in essence, a handyman who cares for the horses and supervises the groundskeepers. Also, because of my physical condition, his duties include helping me with tasks I can no longer do myself. Daphne Morgan has run this household for as long as I can remember. She rules with an iron fist but she is well-loved by all the staff. Calvin Hensley is my driver. He's a bit simple but a nicer fellow you will never meet. Hattie is the cook and Gretchen assists her in the kitchen. You will never go hungry while they are preparing the meals. Millie and Betsy are the maids. You will be hard pressed to find a speck of dust in this house with those two around. Each of our servants has a room on the first floor. I hate to think what will happen to them when I pass and they go their separate ways. They are like family to each other. Samantha was fascinated when he told her about his great-great-grandfather and how he built the town from nothing. An hour later, Samantha apologized for keeping him so long.

"No, dear, you needn't apologize. I have enjoyed our conversation immensely. Your parents must be very proud of you because you are a delightful young woman. If you think you can put up with a decrepit codger like me, I would like to hire you as my personal assistant." Samantha was so pleased that she almost jumped out of her chair. Her instinct was to hug this man who seemed to be the answer to her prayer. She did restrain herself and simply smiled and thanked him for the opportunity.

"It's time for my nap now," he said. "You will find I nap often during the day. That will give you time for yourself. We dine at six o'clock every evening. After that, you are on your own to be with your friends. I'll call Daphne to show you to your room."

Daphne was kind, but all business as she walked Samantha to her new room on the second floor of the west wing.

The room was beautiful and larger than the downstairs of Samantha's parents' house. She walked into a sitting room with a large fireplace and bookshelves lining one wall. There were an overstuffed sofa and matching chair with a footstool placed in front of a large television. Even though it was a cloudy day, the room was bright and cheerful in pretty yellows with soft green furnishings. Daphne led her into the bedroom. The bed was the largest one Samantha had ever seen. It was so high that there was even a step stool on the side. She had to fight the urge to flop on top of it and kick her shoes off. She had her own private bathroom with a luxurious tub.

"Are you sure this room is for me, Miss Morgan?"

"Very sure, Miss Degan. I'm happy to see it being used. It's been over twenty years since it was the nursery for Professor and Mrs. Stonehill's daughter."

"Professor Stonehill's daughter?" Samantha asked, thinking she must have meant granddaughter.

"Yes, his daughter. I'm sure the professor will fill you in; after all, you are helping him with his memoirs. Her name was Amari. It means miracle because little Mari was truly a miracle." Daphne turned her head as her eyes filled with tears. "I'm sorry. I can't talk about it; it was such a terrible tragedy."

"I'm sorry, Miss Morgan. I didn't mean to upset you."

"It's not your fault, my dear, but please call me Daphne. Miss Morgan sounds so stuffy, don't you think?"

Samantha was given a key to the room and a remote for the fifth stall in the twelve-stall garage. She met Calvin Hensley who was driving one of three limousines into the first stall. He was a friendly older gentleman. He removed his cap and exposed a shiny bald head. He had been the professor's chauffeur for just over twenty years. He seemed anxious to show her all three of the limousines parked in the garages.

"I've just come back from gassing up this one. The Professor doesn't need my services so much anymore. My days aren't nearly as busy as they were when I started here. I was a young man then; I'd just reached my thirtieth birthday and had a hard time finding a job. I was working as a mechanic in a shop downtown. I didn't like it and I wasn't very good at it. In those days, the Professor drove his own car. He had a little red Mustang convertible. You'd think with all his money he'd have some expensive foreign sports car but not the Professor. He once told me it was bad enough he was saddled with that big old mansion and the family limousines. He wanted a nice, normal vehicle that he could drive around town without calling attention to himself.

"He came into the shop one day because he heard a strange noise in the Mustang. I was the only one on duty at the time because my boss was out for lunch. I opened the hood and checked everything I could see. I told him I thought everything was fine. He started to pull away and the transmission fell to the ground.

He got out of the car and walked up to me, saying "You're not much of a mechanic, are you?"

My face must have shown the horror I felt because his next words were, "What kind of driver are you?"

"That I can do, sir."

"Will you drive me home?"

I was reluctant because my old pickup truck didn't seem suitable for this distinguished professor. "I'd be happy to, sir," I said, "that is if you don't mind a ride in old Bessie over there." I pointed to my dilapidated truck.

"I'd be honored to ride in a truck named Bessie. That was my favorite nanny's name when I was a youngster," he laughed.

"I'd never met anyone who'd had a nanny before. In fact, I'd never met anyone who was rich before. I couldn't believe it when I saw where he lived. He had me drop him off right at the front door. He didn't seem to mind that he was in a beat-up old truck. He thanked me for the ride and handed me a twenty-dollar bill. Then he turned back and asked if I'd consider being his chauffeur. I couldn't believe my ears. I'd heard the word *chauffeur* before, but I didn't dream I'd ever be one."

Samantha liked Calvin. He was funny, although he didn't seem to know it.

He told her he would drive her wherever she wanted to go. He also said he'd take care of her little VW and keep her gassed up and running, as he put it.

*****

Samantha couldn't believe her good fortune. She went back to the dorm room that had been home for almost four years. She packed her few belongings and walked away without looking back. She wouldn't miss her roommate, a freshman who'd used their room as a love nest with her boyfriend. She definitely wouldn't miss the communal bathroom or the commotion that went on into the wee hours every night. She almost skipped on her way to her Volkswagen Bug and let out a yelp of joy as she pulled away from the dorm parking lot.

CHAPTER 2

Two months later, Samantha graduated at the top of her class. Professor Stonehill arranged for her entire family, along with the staff of Stonehill Manor, to attend the graduation ceremony, with special seating in the first four rows of the auditorium. It was a large group as Samantha's brothers were married with children of their own. It was a double celebration for the Degan family. Their little sister was receiving her diploma and the very next day their parents would be leaving for the cruise they had planned for years.

A graduation party was held on the lawn of Stonehill Manor. The staff had all grown extremely fond of Samantha. They took pride in showing her family the mansion they cared for so diligently.

Colleen Degan was happy that her daughter was living in such luxurious surroundings, but wondered how she would ever meet a nice young man holed up in a mansion with an eighty-year-old employer and servants who were well into their sixties and older.

"Mom, don't worry about me. I'm enjoying my life here. I suppose because I was the youngest in the family, I'm used to hanging out with older people." She ducked her head as her brother, Dennis, took off his shoe and threw it at her.

"Children, behave yourselves," laughed Colleen.

It was a delightful day for everyone. The Professor skipped his morning and afternoon naps and was ready for bed before seven o'clock. He excused himself and the party went on for a couple more hours.

Samantha was sorry to see her family leave, each going off to their own lives. She wondered, as her mother had, whether she would ever meet someone to share her life with.

*****

The summer passed by quickly for Samantha. She spent hours with the professor, listening to his stories and taking notes. She attended class in the morning, sat with him until his afternoon nap, and then typed her notes while he was resting. At night, she studied for her master's degree.

Samantha didn't mind that she had no friends her age. Her work kept her busy.

The Professor had led a fascinating life. For eighteen years, he was the only child of Hawthorne and Maybelle Stonehill. He arrived home from boarding school after his last year to be greeted by a newborn baby sister. Fenwick didn't know what to make of the little thing. He'd never been around a baby before. His mother encouraged him to touch her tiny hand. He did and she wrapped her little fingers around his. Fenwick fell in love with little Eliza at that very moment.

Fenwick was scheduled to attend college in Boston as his father and his grandfather had done. As he didn't want to leave his baby sister, he begged and pleaded with Hawthorne to let him stay home and finish his education at Lancashire University. With misgivings, Hawthorne finally gave in to his son's request.

Fenwick lived at Stonehill Manor and grew fonder of Eliza by the day. As she grew older, it was obvious she adored her big brother. Fenwick was always there for Eliza to help her repair her doll house or sew her favorite teddy bear's arm back in place. When she became a teenager, it was Fenwick who scrutinized the intentions of the boys who came calling. On Eliza's twenty-first birthday, she met Lynwood Pennington, the son of a prominent North Carolina family. It was love at first sight for the young couple. Fenwick gave his blessing to the couple but was heartsick when his beloved sister moved south after her marriage to Lynwood.

Eliza was enchanted with her new life with Lynwood. The couple traveled all over the world, partly because of Lynwood's business and partly because he had always been a jet-setter and wasn't about to let marriage stand in his way of continuing that lifestyle. Eliza had led a very sheltered life with her aging parents and overprotective brother. She felt like a new person and, although she missed Fenwick, she was thoroughly enjoying her new life with Lynwood.

After ten years of marriage, Eliza gave birth to a baby boy and, eleven months later, another boy.

Life in the Pennington household was chaotic but the couple enjoyed their boys, Bentley and Gilford. They continued to schedule travel times but found they missed their sons too much to stay away for long.

Fenwick visited his sister when he could get away. He was busy throughout the year with his college duties and active social life. He enjoyed being with Eliza's boys. They could be a handful but they were funny and lively.

Fenwick never lacked for female companionship. He wasn't one to boast about his good looks but Samantha had seen enough photographs of him in his youth from the albums in the library to know he would have been quite the catch in his day.

He met Veronica Smythe at a party hosted by her friends, Anna and Walter Donaldson. The party celebrated Professor Donaldson's promotion to full professorship at Lancashire University.

"Fenwick, I would like you to meet my dear friend, Veronica Smythe. Veronica, say hello to Dr. Fenwick Stonehill."

"I'm pleased to meet you, Veronica. Please call me Fenwick; I drop the doctor in social circles. You'd be surprised how many people recite their ailments when they think I'm a medical doctor."

Veronica laughed and said, "I'm pleased to meet you too, Fenwick."

Veronica had beautiful brown hair and piercing blue eyes that captivated him. He fell madly in love with her immediately. The two spent the entire evening together.

Fenwick asked if he could call on her again and she readily accepted.

Veronica and Fenwick became inseparable. Veronica accompanied Fenwick to university functions, they attended local plays and concerts and were often observed having dinner together at local restaurants. Although there was a fifteen-year difference in their ages, they married three months after their first meeting.

The Stonehill Manor staff welcomed Veronica home. They were joyful that the professor had found someone to share his life. Veronica was a warm and happy woman who made it a point to get to know all the staff personally. Fenwick had never known such happiness. The only thing lacking in their idyllic life was a child. Fenwick feared he was too old to father a baby. He and Veronica both visited their doctors but were told there was no reason Veronica could not conceive.

Ten years later, at the age of forty-one, Veronica gave birth to a healthy baby girl. She was their miracle and they named her Amari Joy. They called her Mari for short. From the beginning, Mari showed signs of being a beauty. She had the same piercing blue eyes as her mother. She was pampered and loved by every member of the staff. Fenwick had never been happier. He was madly in love with his wife and madly in love with his baby girl. He had no idea how dramatically his life was about to change in such a horrible way.

CHAPTER 3

It was a busy fall socially for the Stonehills with parties and the opening of the theater season. Fenwick was invited to lecture at prestigious Boston College at the beginning of November. Veronica had never been to Boston and Fenwick was anxious to have her join him. The couple returned home two weeks later.

Calvin and their limousine were waiting at the airport to take them home to Stonehill Manor and their little Mari.

"Oh, Fen darling, I'm so anxious to see our beautiful girl. It seems ages since we were with her. I wonder if she misses us. Please hurry, Calvin. It's getting late, and I don't want Miss Schindler putting her to bed before we get there."

"Calm down, Veronica dear. Calvin is going the correct speed. We don't want a patrolman stopping us and preventing us from getting home in time to see Mari. I spoke to Miss Schindler before we left Boston and she assured me our little girl is awake and waiting for us."

As the limo pulled into the long winding driveway of the mansion, flashing lights could be seen toward the house.

"What's happening?" Veronica cried out.

"Calvin, please hurry! Something is terribly wrong. Step on it man!" Fenwick shouted.

Calvin pulled up to the front door as close as he could. Veronica and Fenwick raced from the limo. A police officer stopped them before they could get to the door.

"Mr. and Mrs. Stonehill?" he asked.

"Yes, Officer, what's happening? Why are you here? What's wrong?"

"I'm afraid I have bad news, sir. Your daughter Amari Joy Stonehill is missing."

"That can't be. We have security; we have servants. They would never let anyone take our daughter. Where is her nanny, Miss Schindler? She would never leave her alone."

"Miss Schindler has been sedated; she was being questioned and became hysterical. A doctor was called to tend to her and he thought it best she receive the sedative."

"I don't care how sedated she, is I want to talk to her. Get her down here now."

"It won't do any good, Fenwick; she will sleep until morning." It was the voice of Doctor Williams. "We need to get Veronica into the house. As you can see, she's in shock."

Fen turned to see his wife staring at the mansion. Her eyes were glazed over and she wasn't moving. Fen rushed over and picked her up, carrying her into the parlor.

Fenwick could hear the servants mumbling and sobbing through the doors to the library. He reluctantly left Veronica and Doctor Williams alone and ran to the library, opening the door and startling the servants.

"Where is she?" he screamed. "Who took my daughter? Bring her back now. I'll give you any amount of money you want. Just bring my baby back." He started to sob himself.

George placed his arm around Fenwick's shoulder. "Come sit down, boss. We've tried to piece together what happened tonight. No one saw any strangers.

Little Mari was in her crib one minute and gone the next. Miss Schindler had gone to the sitting room to warm Mari's bottle. When she returned, not two minutes later, Mari had disappeared."

For the next several weeks, the servants were interrogated again and again. Miss Schindler was relieved of her duties and returned to her home in Wisconsin. Anyone who could be found who had been anywhere near the mansion was questioned. Delivery men were stopped at the door and quizzed. All the Stonehill acquaintances and colleagues of the professor were called in and interviewed.

Most of the students and faculty of Lancashire University and many of the townspeople joined in the search for the little girl.

Veronica was never the same again. She refused to leave the house and eventually refused to leave her bed. She died of heart failure on what would have been Mari's fifteenth birthday.

Fenwick didn't accept the fact that his daughter would never be returned. He believed in his heart that she was still alive. After Veronica's death, he poured his heart and soul into his writing and lecturing. His health began to deteriorate. His muscles weakened to the point that he needed help getting in and out of bed and into his wheelchair. He still lectured at the college several times a year. The lecture hall was always packed when he presented his entertaining discourse. Fenwick Stonehill was a very well-loved but very sad man.

Samantha Degan was a breath of fresh air when she walked into Fenwick's study for the first time. She was young and eager to learn from the elderly man. Her eyes were like saucers when she looked around. It reminded him of the first time Veronica saw Stonehill

Manor. He felt a tear at the corner of his eye and brushed it away. He didn't think Samantha saw it, although she would see many more tears in the months to come.

Mari's nursery suite had never been changed in the twenty years since she was kidnapped. When Veronica was alive and before she became bedridden, she would sit for hours in the room. Fenwick knew it made her feel close to her daughter so he didn't change a thing. After Veronica died, he couldn't bring himself to clear out the room.

When Fenwick talked to Professor Hendricks and the professor suggested he write his memoirs; Fenwick simply laughed at the suggestion.

"No one wants to know about some old washed up professor's life."

"Professor Stonehill, you have led a fascinating life. You have shown courage through all your trials. I know of a young woman who would benefit from listening to you and helping you write the story of your life. I think she is a talented writer."

"I'll consider it," he said with a twinkle in his eye.

One day, Calvin was helping him into the limo that accommodated his wheelchair.

"I've thought about it, Calvin, and I think it's a good idea to write my memoirs even if no one ever reads them. I'll contact Professor Hendricks today about it."

"Right, Professor, it's a grand idea." Calvin had no idea what his boss was talking about but he agreed with him just the same.

*****

Later, Calvin pulled into the driveway and helped Fenwick to his wheelchair and up the ramp beside the front steps.

"Call everyone together and wheel me to Mari's room."

The servants were summoned to the old nursery. Some hadn't ever been in the suite before. Tears began to flow when they opened the door and saw the rooms decorated for a baby girl. Memories of beautiful little Mari came flooding over them.

Fenwick cleared his throat. "This is what we are going to do. These rooms are to be decorated to fit a young woman who will be living here and assisting me in writing my memoirs. I'm partial to pretty yellows and greens but if you think of something better, feel free to go with that if it's bright and cheerful. I want everything new, the walls painted, the fixtures in the bathroom updated, new window dressings, the works. Get the contractors here tomorrow morning. Let's get this thing started. I'm an old man and I don't have all that much time left."

It was a busy time. A decorator was called that very afternoon. She arranged for a contractor who had an excellent reputation. She gave him fair warning that the job was to be done perfectly and quickly or it would be his head as well as hers. She shopped in the most exclusive shops she could find within a one-hundred-mile radius of the mansion. No expense was spared.

By the end of the second week, the professor was getting anxious.

"When is that confounded woman going to be done with the room? I have an interview on Tuesday with a young woman who was highly recommended by Professor Hendricks. I can't have her living in an incomplete suite, now can I?"

"I'll check with Ms. Reardon, sir. I do believe she is putting some finishing touches on the rooms today."

George didn't mind seeking out Ms. Reardon. He was rather smitten with her. He liked watching the way her red hair bounced when she walked. She wore the tallest high heels he had ever seen and the shortest skirts.

"George, I'm working as quickly as I can. We will be done by tomorrow afternoon. I wish your employer would stop by to approve what we're doing. There won't be time to finish the job by Tuesday if he wants changes."

"I think it looks fine, Ms. Reardon." George smiled at her.

Ms. Reardon rolled her eyes. *The big oaf doesn't know a thing about décor,* she thought to herself.

The following afternoon, Professor Stonehill wheeled himself to the elevator and exited on the second floor. The truth was, he didn't want to see the room decorated in anything but as a nursery. He felt disloyal to Mari and Veronica. He opened the door slowly and took a deep breath. There was no sign of the former nursery suite. The last reminders of Mari were gone. He wanted to shout out for his baby girl, but instead followed closely behind Ms. Reardon as she proudly showed off her work.

"Very nice job. I'm sure our new tenant will be happy here."

Fenwick knew Ms. Reardon expected more praise but it was the best he could do. He would give her a nice bonus, to make up for the disappointment he saw on her face.

*****

Samantha settled into her life in Stonehill Manor. Her sessions with the professor were her favorite part of her day. She listened intently and took notes. He made her laugh and cry with his stories. She fretted that she wouldn't be able to capture the uniqueness of the man on the pages of a book.

Samantha was with him when he received a call from his nephew that his sister, Eliza had succumbed to cancer. Having lost their father the year before, the nephews were now the only family Fenwick had left in the world.

The physical effort to attend Eliza's funeral was more than Fenwick's doctor would allow. He grieved her loss and shared his memories of her with Samantha. He had her reach into his closet to find a file box marked with Eliza's name. Each section was marked with a year. Samantha was able to see Eliza from the time she was an infant all through the years until the last year of her life. There were pictures of every stage of the boys' lives too. They were both very handsome. The family resemblance was remarkable. Samantha thought they looked a lot like their maternal uncle did in his younger days.

"Those two are real rascals," he chuckled. "They have taken over Pennington Industries, but they leave the day to day running to their assistants. It takes time but we Stonehills do settle down eventually." He had a twinkle in his eye and Samantha knew he was thinking of another story to tell her. Although it was a sad day, a happy conversation helped Fenwick deal with the loss of his sister.

Approximately two weeks before his murder, the professor seemed to become more pensive than usual.

"Professor, are you feeling well? You are uncharacteristically quiet and I haven't heard any of your wonderful stories in days."

"I'm fine, dear, there is something that is troubling me but until I can get some answers, I'd rather not talk about it."

Samantha didn't ask about his mood again but she was concerned.

CHAPTER 4

Samantha sat in the back seat of the police car driven by the detective who had handcuffed her earlier. She couldn't get the vision of Professor Stonehill's lifeless body out of her mind. If only she had checked on him earlier. If only Judy Pryor hadn't had a sick child and left him to fend for himself. Who would stab the professor with his own letter opener? It didn't make any sense; everyone loved the professor. Did he interrupt a burglary in progress? That didn't make sense either; no one could break through the security in the mansion even if they tried. Although, apparently, someone must have broken through twenty years ago when little Mari was taken from her crib.

The car came to a halt in front of the police station. Detective Wells opened the rear door.

"Do you need help getting out of the car, Ms. Degan?"

Samantha shook her head, but couldn't say the words. Detective Wells seemed like a nice person. At least she seemed much nicer than that other guy, Fletcher. She didn't like him at all.

An officer led her to a room with a table and some metal chairs. *This is nothing like Stonehill Manor*, she thought to herself, and wished she were back there listening to the professor regale her with his stories.

She sat down on a chair, felt a chill and wished she'd brought a sweater. The sun was coming through a crack in the blinds, providing some light in an otherwise drab room. Samantha attempted to move toward the light but didn't have the strength to budge her chair.

The door opened and, unfortunately, it was Detective Fletcher.

She heard the other detective tell him to be gentle with the woman. "It's obvious she's in shock, Fletch. Be careful or you'll lose the case before you even start."

He frowned slightly at Robin Wells and looked Samantha in the eye.

"Why did you kill Professor Stonehill, Ms. Degan?"

Alarmed, Samantha finally found her voice, "I didn't kill him, I was trying to help him. He had a letter opener stuck in his back." She could feel the bile rising in her throat as she tried to erase the picture of that letter opener protruding from the professor's back.

"Were you and the professor lovers?" Detective Fletcher snarled.

"No, of course not. That's a terrible thing to say. Professor Stonehill is a gentleman."

"Why were you living in his house? You're a young woman; what would make you want to live in that big mansion with an old man?" he snapped accusingly.

"Professor Stonehill hired me to help him write his memoirs. Part of my compensation included room and board"

"How much were you paid for your services, Ms. Degan?"

"Why do you want to know that? What difference does it make? What are these questions all about? Do I need a lawyer?" she asked.

"Do you think you need a lawyer?" the detective sneered.

Detective Wells put her hand on Detective Fletcher's arm. "If Ms. Degan would like to call her lawyer, it's her right."

"I don't have a lawyer. I don't know who I would call."

"We can give you the name of a public defender, Ms. Degan."

At that moment, the door opened.

"Here's the coroner's report, Fletch."

"Thanks, Dennis."

Detective Fletcher opened the envelope, read the report and pointed to something written there and handed it to Detective Wells.

"Looks like the victim died two hours before you were caught holding the murder weapon in your hand. Did you change your mind after you'd done the deed, Ms. Degan?"

"No. I didn't kill him. I told you I was trying to help him."

"We're going to have to let her go Fletch."

Detective Fletcher's brows narrowed. He glared at Samantha accusingly. She could feel his dislike for her and it made her shiver.

"I can't hold you, Ms. Degan, but that doesn't mean you're off the hook. I think you killed the professor and I'm going to prove it."

He stormed out of the room, leaving Detective Wells alone with Samantha.

"Why does he hate me so?" she asked.

"Fletch has been hardened as a detective. He worked the streets of Chicago for a few years before coming here. He's seen more senseless killings than you and I can imagine. Our investigation isn't over, Ms. Degan. If you're innocent, Detective Fletcher will be the first to admit his mistake in accusing you of murder."

That didn't make Samantha feel any better. Riding back to the mansion in the patrol car, she wondered if she had any right to be back there. Poor Professor Stonehill no longer needed her services.

George and Daphne met her at the front door.

"Dear Samantha, come in and let me fix you a cup of tea. You've been through such a terrible ordeal," Daphne soothed.

The warm reception surprised Samantha. When she was escorted out of the house earlier in the day, the entire staff was staring at her as though she was a murderer.

"I didn't kill the professor, Daphne. I swear I didn't."

"Of course, you didn't," said George. "We were all in shock, so please forgive us for our reaction. We know you couldn't have hurt the professor. Whoever killed him won't get away with it."

"I'm the only suspect, aren't I?"

"So far there are no other leads. The police have questioned the staff to no avail. They haven't found evidence that a stranger entered the mansion. I can't believe one of our own is responsible for this tragedy."

Daphne came back into the room with a cup of tea. Samantha held the cup in both hands; she'd been cold ever since early this morning when she'd found the professor slumped in his wheelchair.

The rest of the staff came into the room to offer her support and tell her they knew she was innocent. There were tears and sadness over the death of their beloved professor and the uncertainty of their lives that lay ahead.

CHAPTER 5

"Fletch, you have a phone call. Somebody named Bentley Pennington. He says he's that professor's nephew."

Fletch picked up the phone reluctantly. He didn't want to talk to some relative who would no doubt ask why someone hadn't been arrested in the case of the murdered professor.

"Joseph Fletcher here; what can I do for you, Mr. Pennington?"

"You can tell me why my uncle's killer hasn't been arrested. What's wrong with you people? My lawyer tells me you caught the murderer red-handed. I want answers, detective, and I want them now."

Joseph Fletcher was not a patient man. He forced himself to breathe slowly before answering the question.

"Mr. Pennington, we have not made an arrest because we can't prove the suspect you are talking about killed your uncle. The investigation is still underway."

"That won't do, detective. My brother and I are flying to Lancashire later this afternoon. I expect a full report on that little tramp who offed our uncle."

"I look forward to meeting with you, sir," Fletch lied.

*****

"Samantha, the Pennington brothers will be here this afternoon," said Daphne. "Oh, you're going to love the professor's nephews. They are so charming and witty and such a delight to have around. I'm sure they will brighten up the place even though the circumstances are so distressing."

While Daphne spoke, Samantha was packing her few belongings. She wasn't sure where she would go. She'd saved some money from her generous salary and thought she could find a room off campus until she finished her studies.

"I'd like to meet them, but I should be on my way to find a place to live. I kept my notes and I'll work on the professor's memoirs as I get a chance. I only wish he was still here to help me with the finished product."

"You can't leave," Daphne exclaimed. "The professor wouldn't want that. You were very important to him, Samantha, and surely his nephews will want you to stay on too."

"I doubt they will want a stranger taking up space here. I will stay long enough to meet them. I'm sure they have questions for the person who found their uncle's body."

*****

"George, we can't let Samantha move out. This old place will never be the same without her."

"Daphne, this old place is not the same with her or without her now that the professor is gone. You know there's no need for us to stay on here either. The Penningtons will probably sell the mansion. After all, their lives are in North Carolina. In the meantime, Adam Green, Professor Stonehill's lawyer, is on his way over. Maybe he'll have some answers for us."

"Oh, George, we're a family here. I can't believe we must go our separate ways after all these years," sighed Daphne as she dabbed her eyes. "It's difficult enough losing the professor but losing our home too, it's just not fair."

The doorbell rang, announcing a visitor. George led Mr. Green into the parlor.

"George, my dear fellow, I am sorry to be making a call under these circumstances. Professor Stonehill left interim instructions regarding his wishes for the staff upon his death. The reading of his last will and testament will take place later. Kindly gather everyone and I will reveal the directives."

The staff in residence gathered in the large parlor. They were all anxiously waiting for Mr. Green to read the list of instructions left by the professor. There was a collective sigh of relief when they were told nothing would change. They were to continue with their duties as usual. The professor's day and night nurses were to be given a generous severance pay. He specifically requested that Samantha stay in the residence and complete his memoirs.

*****

There was no time for celebration, however, as the Pennington brothers were due to arrive in just two hours. There were meals to prepare, guest suites to dust and freshen, and beds to be made. The prospect of the professor's nephews visiting the mansion was enough to change the somber mood to one of anticipation and joy.

Everyone waited at the door when they heard Calvin pull the limo up to the front steps. Samantha peeked over George's shoulder at the two handsome brothers as they walked up the stairs. Instead of smiling faces and laughter, both men were scowling.

"Good afternoon, everyone," said Bentley. "Now get on with your duties. This is not a social call."

The brothers both stared directly at Samantha. She could feel a shiver going through her. She began to turn and follow the others out of the vestibule, when she heard Bentley call her name.

"Ms. Degan, my brother and I would like to have a word with you in private."

George put his hand on Samantha's shoulder.

"I said, in private, George."

Bentley pointed to the library and the three of them walked into the room. Gilford closed the door behind them.

"They do know Samantha is innocent, don't they, George?" asked Daphne.

"It wouldn't seem so, would it?" he replied.

*****

"Ms. Degan, suppose you tell my brother and me just what your duties were around here," Bentley said bluntly.

Samantha's face turned red. "I was Professor Stonehill's personal assistant. He was in the middle of writing his memoirs before his tragic death."

"Doesn't it seem strange to you that an eighty-year-old man would invite a young girl into his home and set her up in his daughter's bedroom? Tell me, how much was he paying you for your services?"

"Mr. Pennington, I'm sure you are grieving for your uncle as we all are. I will overlook your rudeness toward me, but I think you should have more respect for your uncle. Professor Stonehill was a wonderful, kind and loving man. He didn't need to buy affection as you seem to suggest."

"Tell me this then, why would a young girl like you want to live in this uptight old mansion with nothing but over-the-hill servants and an elderly crippled man?"

"First, I'm not a young girl. If you must know, I am working on my master's degree. The professor was not only my employer, but my mentor. I have learned more from him in the last six months than I did in four years of college. I happen to like the over-the-hill servants, as you put it; they have shown me nothing but kindness and compassion, unlike you, Mr. Pennington."

"Ben, I think you've gone too far." Gilford finally found his voice. "Ms. Degan seems like a nice person, maybe she isn't after Uncle Fen's money after all. May we call you Samantha?"

"You can call me anything you want. I will be out of here in five minutes. In fact, I'm already packed."

"Don't be so hasty. I'm sorry if I came down hard on you, Samantha. I had to make sure you weren't taking advantage of our uncle. Why don't you tell us why you were found holding the weapon that killed him?"

"I agree you should know how your uncle died. As I have told the police, I found him with the letter opener embedded in his back. All I could think of was relieving his pain. I was so shocked that I couldn't comprehend the fact that he might be dead. I pulled the letter opener out of him, trying to help him but it was too late. He'd been dead for a couple of hours according to the coroner. If you'll excuse me, I'll be on my way."

"Don't go, Samantha," said Gilford. "We'd like to get to know you. We would love to help you with Uncle Fen's memoirs. Please forgive Ben for his callousness."

Samantha glanced at Bentley.

"I'd like you to stay too. I think I might have misjudged you. Can we forget about my tirade? I'm so embarrassed I acted that way."

"I understand you are mourning and I won't take your remarks personally. Now, if you will excuse me, I have work to do in my room."

Samantha left the library and closed the door on the way out. Daphne had told her how good-looking the brothers were and she wasn't exaggerating. She didn't much care for Bentley after the way he spoke to her but he was certainly easy on the eyes.

*****

"What do you think Gil?"

"I think she's guilty as sin, but she is a looker. Old Uncle Fenwick always did have good taste in women."

"Next time you can play the bad guy. I think I ruined my chances with her. I hope she's the forgiving type."

"What's wrong with you, Bentley? She killed our uncle and you're thinking of making a move on her?"

"Maybe she killed him, maybe she didn't. I just know one thing. Uncle Fenwick died a happy man."

CHAPTER 6

The funeral service for Professor Fenwick Stonehill was like a national holiday in Lancashire. Classes at the university were canceled; the public schools were closed for the day; all flags were flown at half-staff and the local television station covered the entire observance. Mayor Richard Delaney and Governor Harold Keaton delivered eulogies. The Professor was lowered into the ground beside his beloved Veronica.

Detectives Fletcher and Wells attended the service. Detective Fletcher remained unconvinced of Samantha Degan's innocence.

"Look at her, Robin," he whispered. "You'd think she really cared. See those crocodile tears? She's a skilled actress all right."

"Fletch, why in the world have you taken such a dislike to that girl? She's really very sweet."

"She's really got you fooled, hasn't she? She took a job with the old man so she could wheedle her way into that mansion. Don't tell me she doesn't like that life. She's still living there, isn't she? I can't stand people who take advantage of their good looks just to con some old guy out of his money."

"You're admitting she's good-looking. Maybe that's what's got you all fired up. You're attracted to her, aren't you? The guy who has sworn off women for life is falling for Samantha Degan."

"Shut up, Wells. Just because you're nuts about your guy, you think everyone should hook up with someone.

Well, if I'm going to hook up with anyone, it won't be a conniving murderer like Ms. Samantha Degan."

"You don't believe she's a murderer any more than I do. She's a very nice person, Fletch. If you just looked beyond your resentment toward women, you might see that for yourself."

"What are you talking about? I don't resent you and you're a woman."

"You tolerate me because you have to. I know you'd prefer some macho guy as your partner but you're stuck with me."

That's not true, Fletch thought to himself. He actually liked Wells but she wasn't like any other women he'd known. She was honest; and she didn't pretend to be anything but what she was. He didn't have romantic feelings for her, after all, she was married to someone he liked and respected. They were friends and partners; he knew he'd give his life for her and she would do the same for him. It was ridiculous that anyone would think he was attracted to Samantha Degan. He didn't like her type, the always innocent type, Rachel's type.

He tried not to think of Rachel. She had been out of his life for four years now, but she refused to leave his mind. She was everything he'd ever dreamed of. She was beautiful and smart and funny and, as it turned out, unfaithful. He'd had the ring in his pocket the night she told him she was marrying Reggie Crenshaw. Reggie was a sixty-five-year-old playboy who'd lived off his family's money all his life. Rachel had met him at a party that she'd attended alone while Fletch patrolled the streets of Chicago.

"Fletch, I'm marrying Reggie but we can still see each other. Don't you see, he can give me things that you can't. You're a cop. You can't expect me to choose that life when I can have everything if I marry Reggie. You want me to be happy, don't you?"

"But you love *me*," he said, pleadingly.

"Yes, I do and I always will. Reggie's an old man; I give him another five years, tops. After he dies, I'll be a wealthy woman and we can have a wonderful life together. If only you're patient, my darling."

Fletch turned and walked away in pain and disgust. He threw the diamond ring he'd scrimped and saved for into the Chicago River. He vowed he'd never fall for another woman again. After four years, he'd kept his vow. Why was he having doubts about it now?

*****

Fletch watched as Samantha was led up the aisle of the church on the arms of the rich boys, Bentley and Gilford Pennington. What kind of wimpy names were those? Bentley and Gilford. They were of the same ilk as Reggie Crenshaw. He wondered which one Samantha would end up with, maybe both. She turned his stomach and, yet, he found her appealing.

*****

Adam Green scheduled the reading of the will the day after the funeral in Professor Stonehill's library. Samantha told Daphne she would stay in her room out-of-the-way. She didn't want to interfere with family business.

"I'm sure the professor has left you something, dear. You know how fond he was of you. I think you should be there."

*****

Adam Green methodically read the professor's last wishes. He left generous amounts of money to all the staff and the assurance that they would have a home in the mansion for as long as possible.

Finally, Mr. Green read the names of Bentley and Gilford Pennington. Each of his nephews was bequeathed half of the professor's shares in Pennington Industries. Samantha Degan was left Stonehill Manor, its entire contents and the property surrounding it, in trust along with a sealed envelope.

"That can't be right!" she cried out. "Why would the professor leave me his family home? I can't accept it."

Bentley and Gilford grimaced at her words. She was the best actress either one had ever seen.

"These are the professor's wishes. He knew what your response would be, Samantha, and there is an explanation in this letter."

Samantha took the letter and went directly to her room.

*****

Dearest Samantha,

I know you will think it odd of me to have left you Stonehill Manor. The reason will become clear to you in this letter.

Although my nephews are both bright and amusing, I am aware they have no interest in the Stonehill legacy. You, however, know the importance of its history.

I have shared my most personal thoughts with you while you have assisted me with my memoirs. I do believe you understand the depth of my feelings about family and the Stonehill name.

I know I am asking more of you than I should, but I trust you completely in this matter. I have had a suspicion of late that my beautiful baby girl, Amari Joy, is alive and living her life away from her rightful place in Stonehill Manor. I beseech you to investigate that possibility. I have arranged an open-ended bank account to aid in your efforts.

I have also had a premonition that my death is impending. I don't want to be maudlin but I must prepare myself to meet my maker.

I will understand if you do not wish to accept the challenge of finding my Mari and will not fault you for that decision.

Samantha, you have brought light into this old man's last days. You are truly a gifted young woman and will go far in this life.

Yours most sincerely,
Fenwick Stonehill

*****

Samantha read and reread the letter. How on earth could she go about finding a woman who had been taken as a baby over twenty years ago? What was the professor thinking? Samantha was not a sleuth. This is an impossible task. While the professor merely made a request that she do this, he also gave her an out. But how could she let him down? He had faith in her. She would have to figure out a way to find Amari Joy Stonehill.

CHAPTER 7

"If there was ever any doubt, brother, our little Miss Samantha is definitely a con artist. She might have won this round but she can't outsmart us."

"Gil, she did seem as surprised with Uncle Fen's gift as we did. Maybe she didn't expect it after all."

"Sure she did. Did you see those doe eyes, Ben? She's a fake and a phony. We've come too far; I think it's time we put on the charm. It doesn't matter which one of us she marries, we have to get the mansion back in the family."

"It will be a sacrifice, little brother, but I'll volunteer to marry the vixen. I'd like to charm that innocent smile off her beautiful face."

"Nope, it's gotta be me. You blew it when you came down hard on her the other day."

"Put your money where your mouth is. We'll both give it a try. I'll bet I'm the one she falls for."

"You're on! Let the games begin."

They both laughed as each one of them pictured themselves in the arms of the lovely Ms. Samantha Degan.

*****

"Samantha, dear, are you all right? I know it was a shock to you, finding out you're now the owner of the mansion. I think it's wonderful that the professor entrusted you with his home. However, the brothers Pennington are none too pleased, I can assure you." Daphne chuckled at the thought of the professor outwitting those two rascals.

"I'm sure they aren't happy with me owning Stonehill Manor, and I don't blame them. I'm hoping someday soon the professor's intentions will be clear.

"Will you help me make the staff understand that things will not change around here? There are still tasks to do and meals to prepare. Everyone will carry on as they always have," declared Samantha.

"I'm also wondering when the charming Detective Fletcher will be arriving at the door to question me further once he finds out about the inheritance. The Professor didn't do me any favors, Daphne."

"The Professor always had a reason for what he did. I'm sure there was a reason for this too. He would never want to put you in an uncomfortable position."

"He didn't intend to be murdered either."

Just then, George stepped into the room. "Samantha, Detectives Fletcher and Wells are here to speak with you."

Samantha smiled at Daphne. "I'll be right there, George. Will you ask them to wait in the library please?"

*****

"Good afternoon, detectives, I can't say I'm surprised to see you."

"I'm sure you're not," Fletch practically growled. "Nice profit for a few months' work," he said, glancing around the room.

"My ownership in Stonehill Manor is only temporary, I assure you. I have no intention of reaping any benefits from its sale if that's what you are implying."

"In the meantime, you are living well. Tell me, how are the memoirs coming along? Can we expect to find a copy on the bookstore shelves anytime soon?"

"Professor Stonehill's life was long and very complicated. It will take months before his story is published. If you are through badgering me, Detective, may we get on with your interrogation?"

"Why so nervous, Ms. Degan? Do you have something to hide?"

"Only my lack of patience, Detective Fletcher. I don't mean to be rude, but unless you have good reason to be here, George will show you the door."

"You certainly have taken over as mistress of the manor. Tell me, is it a part you have rehearsed for?"

"That's enough, Fletch," said Robin. "Ms. Degan, we would like to speak with all the staff again. I'm sure you would like to know who is responsible for Professor Stonehill's murder. May we have your permission to question each one again?"

"Of course, you may. Calvin has driven Hattie to town; she likes to choose her own vegetables at the supermarket. I believe everyone else is available. I'll have George round them up."

*****

They decided Robin would do the questioning because she was gentle, and people tended to speak more freely with her. Fletch quietly followed Samantha to the professor's suite on the third floor.

Samantha reluctantly opened the door. There were no signs of the violence that had taken place in the rooms, but Samantha cringed when she glanced toward the desk where the professor had died. She knew it would be a good idea to replace all the furnishings in the rooms but she couldn't bear the thought of discarding everything that reminded her of the professor.

She heard Detective Fletcher clear his throat and looked toward the door.

"What are you doing here? Don't you have some browbeating to carry out downstairs?"

"Robin can handle it. I thought I'd have a look around these rooms again."

"Do you have a warrant?"

"Do I need one?"

"I guess not. I'd like to find out who did this to the professor as much as you would. I know you think I killed him but I didn't."

Fletch didn't want to admit it, but he was beginning to doubt her guilt. He observed that she didn't seem comfortable in her new role as lady of the manor.

"Where are Tweedle-dee and Tweedle-dum this morning?"

"If you are referring to the Pennington brothers, they are still in their rooms. It's only nine thirty; we don't usually get to see them until, at least, eleven o'clock."

"It's amazing that they are able to run a corporation with that kind of schedule."

"Maybe they delegate. Isn't that a sign of a good manager? Don't let me keep you from your work. Go ahead and snoop all you want."

Samantha sat at the professor's desk. She would try to get some work done although Detective Joseph Fletcher was more than a simple distraction. She opened the top drawer of the desk. Something was caught in the slide. She felt around with her hand and was able to dislodge a piece of an envelope.

"Detective, this might not be anything, but I just found this in the drawer slide," she said as she held the scrap in the air.

"What did you find?" Fletch said, trying to ignore the faint smell of her perfume filling the air as he stepped toward her.

"It's from a manila envelope. I haven't been at this desk since the day the professor died. I'm the only one who ever opened his mail. I don't remember seeing a manila envelope. Not only that, the professor was very fastidious; he would never have left a scrap of paper inside a drawer."

"It's not much to go on, but more than we had before." He carefully placed the scrap into a plastic bag and sealed it.

"You know my fingerprints are all over that scrap."

"I know," he smiled

"Detective, why do you dislike me so much? Is it just because you think I'm a cold-blooded killer?"

"My job isn't to like you or dislike you. My job is to find the professor's murderer."

"Well then, don't let me stop you from doing your job."

"Tell me, why did you start working for the professor? Was it only the money?"

"Of course, it was partly the money. I needed a place to live and this job came with room and board. I expected the room to be in the servant's quarters. I knew the professor by reputation, as everyone else in Lancashire did. I'd been to several of his lectures. Helping him write his memoirs was a dream job for me. It also gave me an opportunity to finish my education without burdening my parents with more expense."

"So the relationship was purely boss and assistant, nothing more?"

"Detective Fletcher, are you again insinuating that the professor and I were lovers?"

"Well, were you?"

"You're disgusting. No, we were not lovers. The Professor was a proud and honorable man and I am not the type, I can assure you."

"He might have been proud and honorable, but he was still a man and you are pretty easy to look at."

"I think that's enough of this conversation. Tell me what made you so cynical? Are you this way with all women, or is it just me?"

"Not all women; my partner Robin's a straight arrow. I watched as my grandfather was outsmarted by a nurse our family hired to watch out for his safety. She talked him into turning over what little money he had and then she took off, leaving him with nothing. He lost his house and ended up a broken man in a nursing home. Now take this situation. You work for the professor for a few months, he's killed and you end up owning his estate. Doesn't that seem more than a little suspicious to you?"

Samantha had to admit it sounded more than a little suspicious.

"You might not believe me, but as I told you before, my ownership is only temporary. I can't tell you any more than that."

"If you are holding back information that will help us solve this case, I suggest you share it immediately."

"It has nothing to do with the case. It's something the professor asked me to do for him. I just don't know where to start. I think I've said enough. Please finish your search and let me get back to my work."

*****

Fletch left her alone in the suite and rejoined Robin in the library as she was finishing her questioning of the kitchen maid. *Samantha is holding back something that could be important. I'm going to have Robin talk to her, she might get her to spill the beans,* he thought to himself.

"How'd it go?" Fletch asked.

"I didn't get anywhere. I think we should talk to the night nurse, Judy Pryor. The agency tells me she's working for an elderly woman now. She and the killer were the last people to see the professor alive. She might know something."

"Do you suspect her?"

"No, she's a single mother of three, her husband died a few years ago. The agency confirmed that they've never had a complaint about her. She has no criminal record and it doesn't appear she has a motive."

"Our Ms. Degan, however, has motive and opportunity. She's holding something back. I want you to see if you can get her to open up."

"You're attracted to her; I can tell, Fletch. But I'll be glad to talk to her. I think she's exactly what she seems. I'm sure that's why the old man trusted her with this mansion. It speaks volumes that he didn't want his nephews taking it over after his death."

"Yeah, those nephews don't seem to have anything to do with Pennington Industries. It's time to investigate the status of their company. Let's get back to the station. Which reminds me, I want to run a fingerprint check on this scrap of paper."

CHAPTER 8

"Don't you ever have any fun?"

"You startled me, Bentley. What are you talking about?"

"I asked if you ever had any fun. Since Gil and I arrived in town, you've been slaving away at your computer or worrying about Uncle Fen's staff. You need to get out and enjoy yourself, that is, if you know how."

"What does that mean?" Samantha tried to hide her irritation, although there was some truth to what Bentley was saying.

"Just look outside. It's a beautiful day for a ride in the countryside. I seem to remember a quaint little restaurant off Route forty-six. It's dark and quiet. We could have a couple of drinks and see where the rest of the afternoon leads us."

"It sounds fascinating," she said with a scowl. "I'll have to take a rain check though as I'll be leaving in a few minutes to attend a lecture at the university."

"Bummer! I'll tell you what, I'll go with you. I can't remember the last time I sat through some long-winded professor talking about something that held no interest for me."

"Well, I *am* interested. And now, if you will excuse me, Calvin is waiting to drive me to the university."

"It didn't take long for you to fit right into the affluent life of limos and servants, did it?" he sneered.

"Not that it's any of your business, but Calvin would have nothing to do if he didn't drive the staff and me to town. I would prefer to drive myself in my car, but if I did, there would be no reason to keep Calvin on here."

Samantha walked down the stairs to her suite. She gathered her purse and a notebook. She wondered when the Pennington brothers would be departing and reflected that it wouldn't be soon enough to suit her. Didn't their business need them? Bentley had hit a nerve when he'd asked if she ever had fun. She couldn't remember the last time she'd been out for an evening. With school, work and her writing, it didn't leave much time for a social life.

She ran down the stairs and out to the garages. Calvin had the motor running and held the door open for her.

"Mr. Pennington, what are you doing?" she cried when she discovered him already seated in back.

"I'm going with you. Calvin knows the way to that restaurant and will drive us there after your lecture."

"I'm not going anywhere after the lecture. Please get out of the car. I'll be late if we don't leave now."

"Stop arguing with me and let's go or you will be late."

Calvin looked questioningly at Samantha.

"Go ahead, Calvin. I guess Mr. Pennington will be riding with us."

"You're too uptight; you need to relax." Bentley placed his hands on her shoulders and began to massage them.

"Get your hands off me!" Samantha snapped.

"Everything all right back there, Miss Samantha?"

"Everything's fine, Calvin." She glared at Bentley.

When they got out of the limo, Bentley took her arm protectively. She shook it off.

"I'm perfectly capable of finding my way into the building." Samantha knew she was being overly unpleasant, but this man brought out the worst in her.

He didn't try to touch her again. They walked into the lecture hall and found seats near the podium.

"How am I going to sleep when we're so close to the speaker? Let's move back, I see some empty seats in the last row."

"Feel free to move to one of them. I'm perfectly comfortable here."

All through the lecture, Bentley made cracks about the speaker and about the girl in front of them who played with her ponytail throughout the presentation. Samantha had to nudge him three times because he was falling asleep and threatening to snore loudly.

"I give up," she said during the intermission. "I can't concentrate today because I'm worried about what you're going to do next. I'm going to take you up on that drink offer but just remember, you're buying."

Bentley was pleased with the way Samantha was beginning to thaw. He was proud of his prowess with women. However, Samantha was a different sort of female than those whom he was accustomed to seducing. She was way too serious to live in his world. She would be a challenge, but he was sure he could make her fall in love with him. Although it was time he settled down and married, the thought of being tied down to a wife and family made him cringe. He felt a duty to produce a new generation of Penningtons and he'd love to beat his brother to the punch.

Bentley was too thirsty and too anxious to press his perceived advantage to drive out into the country for those drinks. "Just drop us off at the nearest pub, Cal. We'll call when we're ready to come home."

Samantha sat in the booth sipping her wine and feeling the tension leave her body. She knew Bentley was flirting with her but it felt good to have the attentions of a handsome man. She knew his motives had more to do with her ownership of Stonehill Manor than it did with her being irresistible. It didn't matter; she would enjoy every moment of it. She needed a break from the nightmare of remembering the professor's lifeless body and being the prime suspect in his murder.

After her second glass of wine, Samantha took out her cell phone and called Calvin to come pick them up.

"We're just getting started; you can't leave now," Bentley pleaded. He thought he'd been making progress and now, she was ending their time together. Neither one of them noticed the penetrating eyes of Detective Joseph Fletcher as he sat at the bar nursing his draft beer.

He's zeroing in for the kill, Fletch thought as his irritation level rose. *Or maybe they're in this thing together. I suspect the Pennington boys are living off the last of their family's fortune. That might mean that Samantha is as innocent as she looks. That leaves me wondering what her story is? I really don't believe she was the professor's lover, but I can't understand why a young, attractive girl would be satisfied living in that mansion with an octogenarian. Why did the professor leave her that place? What was the real connection between the two of them?* He scowled as Bentley Pennington put his arm around Samantha's waist and guided her out the door.

"You ready for another draft, Fletch?" asked Maggie, the bartender.

"Yeah, one more and then I'll be on my way. Tell me, Maggie, what's going on between those two who just left?"

"Detective Fletcher, if I didn't know better, I'd think you're jealous." Maggie laughed.

"No, I'm not jealous. I'm investigating a crime and I'm pretty sure those two had something to do with it."

"Are you talking about the murder of Professor Stonehill?"

"Maybe, did you know the professor?"

"I haven't seen him in a long time. I heard he was in bad physical shape before he died. He and some of the other professors used to come in here every once in a while. It was back at a time when I was waiting tables. He was the nicest guy, good-looking and friendly. He's the one who encouraged me to become a bartender. I had the biggest crush on him in those days and he didn't even know it. He was madly in love with his wife even though she'd died a few years before. I can't believe someone hated him enough to kill him; he was the greatest."

"It's not always hate that makes someone take the life of another, sometimes it's greed or jealousy or any number of reasons."

"You're not talking about that girl who just left, are you? After all these years behind this bar, I'm a pretty good judge of character. That girl couldn't hurt anyone. The fella is a different story. He and his brother have been in here a few times in the last week or so. They drip with charm and the girls are all over them. I don't trust their type. They come from money but they're real losers in my book."

*****

This is gonna be a piece of cake, Bentley thought to himself. *She's crazy about me.*

"What's next sweetheart? I know a cute little place by the lake where we can get to know each other better."

"You've been here a matter of days and you seem to know a lot about the local drinking establishments."

"I make it my business to discover the charms of whatever city I'm in."

"Calvin, take a right here; the name of the place is The Cozy Cove."

"Calvin, please drop me off at the mansion first. Mr. Pennington is on his own tonight."

"But darlin', the night is just beginning. I can show you a good time; you won't be sorry."

"I won't be sorry because I'm going home." Samantha was relieved when Calvin turned left toward the mansion.

Bentley followed her into the library.

"Thanks for the drinks, Bentley. Now if you will excuse me, I have work to do before dinner."

*****

A disgruntled Bentley dejectedly walked into the hallway to see his brother standing at the top of the stairs grinning.

"Struck out, didn't you, bro? Maybe you'd better step aside and let the real man of the family take a shot at her."

"She was beginning to loosen up. I can't figure her out. She's becoming a challenge and I'm going chip away at that block of ice until she gives in."

Gilford had never known his brother to let a woman get to him like that. Was it possible Bentley had fallen for Samantha? All he needed was his brother going off the deep end for her. The plan was to con her out of the mansion, not mate for life. If it meant one of them would have to marry her, so be it. The marriage would only last as long as it took to gain control of Stonehill Manor and then it would be over. Once they acquired the manor it could be sold to the highest bidder. After that, they'd be able to dump Pennington Corporation and still live life as they'd always lived it.

Gilford poured himself a drink from the bar in the study and walked toward the library. He stopped short when he heard voices.

"Miss Samantha, may I speak with you about something if you aren't busy?"

"Of course, Calvin, come on in. What's on your mind?"

"It's about my niece, well, not really about her, about her school."

"What about her school?" Samantha realized she knew very little about the personal lives of the staff. She'd have to work to rectify that.

"My niece is a teacher at The Melbourne School."

"I've heard of that school. They do wonderful things for children with disabilities. Your niece must be a very special person."

Samantha could see the pride in Calvin's eyes.

"The school has a van that's old and breaks down often. They use the van for transporting the kids to doctors and therapy appointments. I was wondering because the professor's limousine is equipped for a wheelchair, if it would be alright if I helped them out with rides occasionally?"

"Calvin, that's a wonderful idea. You help them when they need you. I am perfectly capable of driving my little bug wherever I need to go."

"Thank you, ma'am. You are most gracious."

Calvin headed for the door when Samantha called him back.

"Calvin, find out how much they would need for a new van and let me know. Make sure it's fully equipped for all of their needs."

Calvin's jaw dropped. "Thank you, Miss Samantha, I'll do that."

Gilford was fuming when he entered the room.

"You don't have the right to fritter away my uncle's money. What are you, some kind of do-gooder? That van you're so willing to buy for some obnoxious kids will cost a small fortune."

"Good afternoon, Gilford. So nice to see you today. Did you just roll out of bed?"

"That's not your business, but it's my business that you are dispensing of Uncle Fenwick's money like it belonged to you."

"If you must know, your uncle left me a generous sum aside from this place. I will be using my money for the van for those *obnoxious kids*, as you call them. Now if you will take your cocktail and find another room to drink it in, I need to get back to work."

Samantha knew she had irritated Gilford, but she didn't care. How could two men, with the same genes as Professor Stonehill, be so different from their uncle?

"Samantha," George said as he knocked on the open door, "Detective Fletcher is asking to see you. He's in the vestibule."

"Could this day get any worse?" she said in frustration. "Ask him to come in, George." Samantha didn't want to admit it, but a little part of her was happy to see him again.

CHAPTER 9

"Detective Fletcher, to what do I owe the honor of your visit?"

"Where's your boy toy?"

"Which one? I have so many. That is, when I'm not murdering my eighty-year-old lover."

Fletch laughed. "I see those drinks have loosened your tongue."

"What drinks? Are you following me?"

"No, I was there first. I saw you and Tweedledum when you came into the pub."

"Actually, I was with Tweedle-dee this afternoon. Is that against the law?"

"No, but maybe it should be. I've done some investigating into the solvency of Pennington Industries. Did you know it's on the brink of bankruptcy? The brothers are mere figureheads who have open-ended expense accounts."

"I assumed as much. The professor always seemed frustrated by their behavior. I hate to see a company go under and have all those jobs lost to the community. Is it really that bad?"

"Yes, it's that bad. My contact tells me there hasn't been any real leadership since the father, Lynwood Pennington, died. The sons are spoiled rich boys who have gambled away most of their inheritance and the rest was spent on fancy cars and fancier women. I thought you should be warned before you became too attached to either one of them."

"Do I look stupid, Detective? I know I'm not worldly like you, but I can tell when I'm being conned. Those boys are after Stonehill Manor. Bentley is playing the romantic part and Gilford is acting as the adversary, although, I don't think it's much of an act on Gilford's part."

"I'm sorry. Samantha, I have underestimated you. Do you mind if I call you Samantha?"

"I don't mind at all. I like it much better than Ms. Degan."

At that moment, Calvin came rushing into the room. "I talked to my niece and she's grateful for your offer. Oh, I'm sorry, I didn't know you had a visitor."

"That's all right, Calvin. Let me know as soon as you complete the deal."

"Detective, Miss Samantha has done the most wonderful thing." Calvin explained the situation with the van to Fletch and then excused himself.

"You're buying a van for those kids with your own money?"

"It's not really my money. The Professor was very generous to all of us. He went a little overboard with me and I'm not comfortable with that much money in my bank account. Those kids need a new van and I'm sure the professor would want them to have one."

"What about this place, are you comfortable owning it?"

"No, I'm not, but I can't disrupt the routine here. I'm hoping a solution will present itself very soon. The Professor asked that I do something for him and I can't figure out how to go about it. I need someone I can trust to talk to and I'm not sure who that is yet."

"Does it have anything to do with his murder?"

"I can't be sure. It's complicated and might not be significant. Detective, dinner will be served in a little while, would you care to join us? That is, unless you're here on official business."

"No, I'm here because I wanted to warn you about the frat boys. You didn't need to be warned after all. I'd like to stay if only to make those two uncomfortable. Please call me Fletch, Samantha. If you'd like to talk to me about what's troubling you, I'd be glad to listen, unofficially, of course."

"Thanks, Fletch," she replied. She liked this new and softer version of the ill-natured detective who seemed bent on charging her with murder.

Bentley and Gilford arrived in the dining room together. They were appalled at the sight of a common police officer sitting at the Stonehill dinner table but forced smiles on their faces.

"Detective Fletcher, what a delight to have you sharing in our family dinner."

It was obvious to Fletch that Bentley Pennington had not stopped at the two drinks he'd shared with Samantha earlier in the day.

"Ms. Degan has graciously offered to feed a public servant and I accepted. I hope you boys don't mind the intrusion."

"Not at all," replied Gilford as he took a generous swallow of his bourbon.

"Samantha dear, why don't you tell my brother of your generosity to the crippled orphans?" Gilford said, slurring his words ever so slightly.

"Gilford, the children at the school are not orphans and not all are crippled, as you so callously put it. They need transportation and I believe the professor would approve of my help in providing a van for their use. I'm planning to pay a visit to the school tomorrow and would be delighted if you and Bentley would join me."

"Count me out," Gilford said as he squirmed in his seat. "I don't like kids, especially crippled ones."

"I'm not hungry," said Bentley as he headed toward the bar. "Samantha, what would you like to drink? You need to loosen up a bit. I think the detective is making you nervous. Isn't he the one who handcuffed you and dragged you down to the police station?"

Samantha ignored the remark and was glad to see both brothers leave the room.

*****

"We've got trouble, little brother," Bentley said when they were out of earshot of Samantha and Fletch. "Those two have something going on between them. Did you see the way they looked at each other? We've got to figure out a way to get rid of the cop if we're to convince the little do-gooder she needs to marry one of us."

"You can have her, bro; she's not my type. I don't like the way she's taken over this place. She acts like she belongs here. Somebody has to set her straight and put her back in her place as a servant, not the mistress of the manor."

"I agree and I'm willing to make the sacrifice. She won't know what hit her when I turn on the charm. She'll forget all about the detective."

"Somehow I don't think it's going to be much of a sacrifice. Just hurry up; I can't wait to get out of this crummy little town. When we were kids, we liked coming here. Uncle Fen was fun back then, before the wheelchair. His crippled body gave me the creeps. I couldn't stand to look at him anymore."

*****

"Those two are plotting something. I can feel it," Samantha declared. "I'm beginning to wonder if they had something to do with the professor's murder."

"I don't think either one of them is smart enough to plan a murder. It wasn't a professional hit unless it was made to look like an amateurish attempt. Are you serious about visiting the school tomorrow?"

"Yes, Calvin's niece called me earlier. She seemed very nice on the phone. She invited me to come and see the facility and meet the children."

"I'm off tomorrow. Would you like some company on the ride up there?"

"Yes, I'd like that. I'll ask Calvin to swing by and pick you up."

"If my neighbors saw me get into a limo in front of my apartment building, they'd think I was on the take. Maybe I'd better pick you up. Do you mind if I drive? I'm not exactly the limousine-riding type."

"I'm not either, but it gives Calvin something to do. It's about an hour's drive from here."

Fletch looked forward to spending time with Samantha. He hated to admit it, but he was growing very fond of her.

CHAPTER 10

It was a beautiful morning and the sun was shining brightly. Samantha woke up in the big overstuffed bed with a smile on her face. She was looking forward to seeing Detective Fletcher again.

She showered and dressed and walked downstairs to the kitchen. She much preferred the cozy atmosphere there instead of eating alone in the massive dining room by herself. It was different when the professor was alive. He always had a story to tell, or an observation to share with her.

This morning, Samantha was ravenous. She filled her plate and, much to Hattie's delight, devoured a generous helping of ham and eggs.

George, who had eaten his breakfast an hour before, announced the arrival of Detective Fletcher.

Samantha grabbed her purse and was out the door. The entire staff watched from the window.

"What's happening?" asked Calvin when he came in from the garage and saw everyone standing by the window.

"Miss Samantha and the detective are on a date," Gretchen reported.

"We don't know if it's a date, Gretchen," admonished Daphne.

"Miss Samantha looked awfully happy and the detective was smiling at her. He didn't look like he was arresting her again."

"I'd have driven them wherever they wanted to go," said Calvin.

"Maybe they didn't want you tagging along on their date, Calvin," giggled Betsy.

Outside, Fletch helped Samantha into his car. "It looks like we have an audience, Samantha. Shall I assure them I'm not taking you to the station?"

"They're all smiling and are probably happy to have me out of their hair for a while."

"They like you, Samantha, it's obvious. I think they are finally beginning to thaw towards me too. They weren't too happy when I hauled you off in handcuffs after the murder."

"I wasn't too happy about it either. I suppose if I saw someone standing over a dead body with a bloody weapon in their hand, I'd have jumped to that conclusion too."

"We will find the killer, I promise you. By the way, that scrap of envelope you found in the drawer had your fingerprints on a corner. It must have happened when you pulled it out of the drawer. I'm guessing the professor didn't want someone to see what was in the report and shoved it quickly into the top drawer of the desk. There were smeared prints but none that could be identified."

"I am trying to remember when, and if, I saw any kind of manila envelope. It was easier for him to use a keyboard than it was to write. He used the computer for all his correspondence."

"Do you think someone was blackmailing him?"

"I suppose anything is possible. However, I don't believe there was ever a hint of scandal about him. I wouldn't be surprised if his nephews have been involved in something either illegal or immoral."

"Here it is a beautiful day and I'm with a beautiful woman talking about extortion and murder. Shall we change the subject?"

"That's a good idea. Tell me about Robin; she seems like a nice person."

"You mean nicer than me?" he laughed.

"I must admit, I liked her right away, especially when you were so mean to me. You thought I'd taken a job with an old man so I could con him out of his money."

"Sorry, I'm such a cynical jerk. Robin is great. She's been on the force for three years now and has been a real asset. Naturally, I threw a fit when she was assigned to be my partner. Not only was she a rookie, she was female to boot. We've already established that I can be a jerk."

"Did you let her know how you felt?"

"Did I ever, but she could take it. She let me gripe and complain and then saved me from being shot in the back by a perp. She's a good detective and a better cop than I am."

*****

The ride to the Melbourne School was a pleasant one. Fletch took the scenic route, away from the busy highway. He liked the idea of being alone with Samantha on the less crowded road. It took longer to get there but neither of them minded.

Samantha told him about growing up with four older brothers, and Fletch talked about his life in the suburbs of Chicago. He didn't know what initially inspired him to be a cop. He wondered sometimes if maybe he'd seen too many detective shows when he was a kid. He remembered his mother's reaction when he told her he was joining the police force. She was sure he would be killed and tried to talk him into selling insurance or used cars, being a banker or a barber, anything but law enforcement.

He'd been a cop for eight years, the first five were in a rough neighborhood in South Chicago. He'd experienced more violence and senseless killings in that five years than he'd ever imagined existed. He'd wanted to give up after his partner was killed in a drive-by shooting but his supervisor told him to take some time off to think about his future. After a month of sitting around feeling sorry for himself, he applied for a job with the Lancashire Police Department. It was not how he envisioned his career, but he found he liked the slower pace of the smaller city.

Samantha admitted that she was torn. Thanks to her inheritance from the professor, she would be able to pursue her writing career without worrying about finances. However, she didn't feel right about spending the money on herself.

"It was like a fairytale when I came to Stonehill Manor. I'd never known anyone who had even one servant, let alone a half-dozen of them. I must admit, I enjoyed the life while the professor was alive. He was the most fascinating man I'd ever known. After he died, I felt out-of-place there. I don't like ordering servants around, although they don't need supervision. They know their jobs and they do them well. If it weren't for them, I'd be tempted to give the place to the Pennington brothers and let them do what they will with it."

"What do you think they'd do with it?"

"They'd sell it, fire the help and fritter away the money. The Professor trusted me with the place and I don't want to let him down. He wrote me a letter, you know, before he died. Somehow he had a premonition that he didn't have long to live."

"Is this about the dilemma you were talking about yesterday?"

"Yes, I thought about it last night and I trust you to help me figure out what to do."

Fletch smiled to himself, he was happy to hear he was on Samantha's mind because he couldn't get her out of his.

"I only hope I can help. What did the professor ask of you?"

"He asked me to find his daughter. She was kidnapped over twenty years ago when she was a baby. She was taken from her crib in the evening hours while her nanny was warming her bottle. I don't think she could be more than twenty-one or two. If the authorities couldn't find a trace of her so many years ago, how on earth will I be able to find her now?"

"Do you think it was wishful thinking on the professor's part that his daughter is still alive?"

"That's a possibility. I only know what Daphne has told me. She still cries when she talks about the baby. If she is still alive, where has she been all these years?"

"I'd heard about the kidnapping before. I think everyone who comes to Lancashire is told the story of the professor's daughter. His wife was younger than he was, so do you suppose she had anything to do with the disappearance?"

"My guess would be no. In fact, it sounds like she might have suffered a nervous breakdown after it happened. I got the feeling they had a beautiful love story. She was hardly an ingénue when Mari was born, as she was in her forties."

"She still could have been a gold digger. Okay, let's assume she didn't have anything to do with the kidnapping, was there a ransom demand?"

"I don't know. The Professor never talked much about the day it happened, or about the aftermath. I do know it was an extremely painful time for him."

"I'll look up the case file when we get back to town, maybe we can find some answers."

*****

The Melbourne School was in a large brick building. The grounds were well-kept but not as impressive as the picturesque Stonehill Manor. Two buildings that resembled barracks were next to the main structure. They were equally uninviting.

Samantha and Fletch walked through the main doors into a dark hallway. The office was on the right, where a friendly young woman in a wheelchair smiled broadly.

"Good morning and welcome to The Melbourne School. Are you Ms. Degan? Amy is expecting you."

"I'm Samantha Degan and this is Detective Fletcher. He was kind enough to drive me here."

A very pretty young woman stepped out of the adjoining office. "Ms. Degan, I'm so happy to meet you, I'm Amy Brooks,"

"Hello, Amy, please call me Samantha." Then she introduced her to Fletch.

"I can't tell you how excited we are for your generosity. The van is being delivered next week. You can't imagine how worried we were that we wouldn't be able to transport the children to where they need to go. Now we will be able to take them on field trips too."

"I'm glad to be able to give you something you need. As I told you on the phone, it's not a gift from me, it's a gift from Professor Stonehill."

Amy showed them all around the school. She explained that she and others on the staff acted as interim administrators as well as teaching classes. The director had a difficult time keeping the administrator position filled. The pay scale at the school was low, too low to raise a family.

"Don't you get government subsidies?" asked Fletch.

"Yes, but even with the subsidies, the cost of keeping these old buildings up to par is enormous. We have a wonderful and dedicated staff here. The children are everyone's top priority."

They met some of the children and Samantha was impressed at how comfortable Fletch was with kids.

After lunch with the teachers and caregivers, Samantha and Fletch left for Lancashire with the promise of returning soon. Amy and the children gathered in the driveway, waving as Fletch pulled away. He glanced at Samantha and saw a tear rolling down her cheek.

"You've done a good thing for those kids, Samantha."

"I just did what I believe Professor Stonehill would have wanted me to do with some of his money. Have you ever seen so much courage from a bunch of children before? They are truly amazing and so are their teachers."

"I agree, I'm happy you invited me along today. Those kids have overcome their limitations with such spirit."

"It makes me more determined than ever to try to find out what happened to the professor's daughter. Do you think I'm being foolish to think I can solve a mystery that took place twenty years ago?"

"I don't know if it's foolish but I'd like to help in any way I can. I will look into the files on the kidnapping in the archives at the station. The department is antiquated enough that cases from that long ago haven't been converted from paper to microfilm or computer yet. I'll start checking this afternoon. It might also help to solve the mystery of who stuck a letter opener in Fenwick Stonehill's back."

CHAPTER 11

Millie Osborne peered out the front window and saw Fletch's car driving toward the house.

"They're back," she cried in glee, "and they're smiling."

"How can you tell if they're smiling, Millie? They're too far away," Betsy Hill chided her.

"They are too smiling; I can feel it."

"Get away from the window, girls. Give Samantha and her beau some privacy," said Daphne as she too happily watched the couple.

*****

"How about dinner tonight since I wasn't able to buy you the lunch I promised?" asked Fletch.

"I'd like that very much," replied Samantha. "You can tell me if you've found anything in the files and I'll question Daphne. I haven't talked to her about Mari because she always cries when the little girl's name is mentioned. Somebody on staff must know something helpful, even if they aren't aware of it."

"You're beginning to think like a detective. I like that. Have you noticed we have an audience?"

"They think we were on a hot date, I'm sure. I don't think I'll mention where we were today. I don't want to remind the Pennington boys that I foolishly squandered their uncle's money."

"Good idea. I'll be back at six." Fletch felt the urge to kiss her but with so many eyes staring at them from the window and the fact that this wasn't really a date, he didn't follow through.

"Hi. everyone," Samantha called out as she walked in the door.

They had scattered but didn't get too far. They responded in unison, "Hello, Miss Samantha."

"I guess we got caught," laughed Daphne. "How was your afternoon?"

"It was very nice, thank you. Daphne, I'd like to ask you some questions. Do you have time to sit in the library with me for a little while?"

"Of course, Samantha. Let me get us some iced tea. You look flushed; it couldn't be because of Detective Fletcher, could it?"

Samantha smiled without saying a word as she walked toward the library.

*****

Daphne carried a tray with tall glasses of tea and cookies on a plate and placed it on the table in front of the sofa. She sat down opposite Samantha.

"Is something wrong, Samantha? Has someone done something to offend you?"

"No, Daphne. I'm trying to think of the best way to approach you on this. I know how upset you get when little Amari's name is mentioned but I need to find out more about the day she was kidnapped."

"The Professor asked you to find her, didn't he?"

"How did you know?"

"I know he never believed she was dead. He did everything he could to find out what happened to her. He hired a private detective but the man told him she simply disappeared without a trace. The police never found any evidence that she was even kidnapped. I'm afraid they suspected the professor and his dear wife of foul play at one time."

"That's impossible," replied Samantha. "The professor would never hurt anyone. How awful that must have been for him. Can you tell me about the day

Mari disappeared? Anything you remember might be helpful, even the smallest detail."

"It was so long ago, but that evening will be engraved in my mind forever. We were having supper in the kitchen. Hattie made chicken and dumplings, one of our favorite dishes. Miss Schindler was with the baby, of course. Gretchen took a tray to the nursery for her. She called for Miss Schindler but she didn't answer. Gretchen thought she was in the restroom and left the tray for her. She walked to the crib and looked down at little Mari who was sleeping peacefully. Gretchen left the room and returned to the kitchen.

"As it turned out, Miss Schindler never did eat her chicken and dumplings. I remember seeing the untouched tray on the table when we ran to the nursery after hearing Miss Schindler screaming that the baby was gone."

"How long after Gretchen left the tray did you hear Miss Schindler?"

"It was thirty minutes or more. The Stonehills were due home at eight thirty. Calvin was scheduled to pick them up at the airport at seven-forty-five. It takes about forty-five minutes to drive home after waiting for the luggage. We were all doing some last-minute sprucing up before they arrived. We liked to make sure there wasn't a speck of dust left on the tables, although they were only interested in seeing their baby. Except for Miss Schindler, everyone was together and accounted for until Calvin left for the airport."

"From what I understand," said Samantha, "Miss Schindler was away from Mari for just a few minutes to warm her bottle. When she returned, the baby was missing from her crib."

"That's the way it happened. She was never the same afterward, the poor girl."

"Did she ever say why she didn't eat the meal that was waiting for her?"

"No, I don't think so, now that I think about it. The tray was gone when the police arrived. Somebody must have taken it to the kitchen in between the time Miss Schindler screamed and the time the police came."

"What do you know about Miss Schindler?"

"She was young, maybe nineteen or twenty. She didn't mingle with the rest of us very much. Of course, her job was to watch over Mari, so she spent most of her time in the nursery. They tried to question Miss Schindler but she was so distraught, she wasn't any help to them."

"Doesn't it seem strange that Miss Schindler didn't hear Gretchen calling her when she brought the tray to the nursery? I'm assuming she used the bathroom that's in the suite."

"I never thought of that before but yes, she should have heard her. You don't think Miss Schindler had anything to do with the kidnapping, do you?"

"I'm not saying she did, but I wonder where she was when it happened." Samantha made a note to herself to look up the full name and last known address of Miss Schindler in the professor's records.

Daphne didn't have much more helpful information but she was trying to remember every detail. She wanted nothing more than to help find out what happened to Mari. She hoped the professor was right, that Mari was still alive.

*****

Fletch drove directly to the station. He was anxious to get started on the investigation into the kidnapping of the professor's baby.

"I thought you had the day off today, partner?" said Robin Wells.

"I do. I'm going to check some old files in the basement archives. Want to help?"

"I love going down there with the mice and spiders. What exactly are you looking for?"

"Information on a twenty-year-old case."

"You must be talking about the Mari Stonehill kidnapping."

"Yes, do you remember it? You were just a kid when it happened."

"I was just a kid but it was the biggest story to ever hit Lancashire. It was the talk of the town for a couple of years. There was constant speculation about who did it. I remember the mother was under suspicion when there was no evidence of an intruder. Some said she accidentally killed the baby and the professor helped her bury the body. It got ugly for a while. They never did solve the case or find the baby."

"When I checked the computer for information on the case, I noticed Chief Paul Clayton's name as the lead investigator."

"They went straight to the top with that one. The Stonehills were the city's most prominent family."

"How about it, Robin? Do you want to help me dig up the old files?"

"Yeah, now you have me curious. I'll go with you but at the first sign of a creepy, crawly thing I'm outta there."

"How can someone who fights off two-hundred-pound criminals be afraid of a little spider?"

"I'm not afraid; I just don't like them," she shivered at the thought.

*****

Fletch was undaunted by the number of file boxes filled with information about the kidnapping. It was obvious the investigation had been thorough even though it had not been solved. He signed out for twenty-three boxes altogether and made three trips with a dolly transporting them back to his office.

"Now what?" asked Robin. "Where do we start?"

"At the beginning, I suppose. But, I don't have too much time today because I'm meeting someone in two hours and I need to get home to take a shower after being in the basement so long."

"Showering for a meeting? Must be more like a date."

"It's not a date, it's just dinner, nothing for you to get excited about."

"It's Samantha Degan, isn't it? I just knew it. I could tell you liked her even though you were accusing her of murder. Has she forgiven you for cuffing her yet?"

"She knows I was just doing my job. I don't want to talk about Samantha now; let's just get to work."

Fletch read the first report of the officer at the scene of the kidnapping.

"This doesn't make sense, Wells. This report would have us believe that the nanny turned her back and someone walked into the nursery and took the baby out of the crib, then walked out the door with it and the nanny never saw this person. It looks like Officer Cummings didn't buy it either. He thought the nanny was must have asleep when it happened. I don't see where they ever got a coherent response from this Ellen Schindler. It says here she had a nervous breakdown after the incident and was admitted to the psychiatric unit of a hospital in Wisconsin. That sounds a little too convenient, don't you think?"

"What are you thinking, Fletch? Are you saying she handed the baby to an accomplice and faked the breakdown?"

"It's possible. It's also possible she knows more than she told Officer Cummings. I'm assuming that's Randy Cummings and I'd like to talk to him."

"Randy's away on vacation in Colorado, the lucky guy. I think he's due back on Monday. He's a good cop. I'm sure he did his best with the nanny under the circumstances."

"I'll talk to him when he gets back. I have to leave now or I'll be late."

"I'll lock your office door when I leave. You've got me interested in this case now, Fletch. I'll keep looking for something we can use. Have fun tonight, lover-boy."

"Tonight is strictly business; we'll be talking about the case.," He smiled as he walked out the door.

CHAPTER 12

Bentley Pennington watched from the window as Fletch opened the door to his car for Samantha.

"She's seeing that Neanderthal again, Gil. I've got to put a stop to that. She'll be giving away more of our money to the widow's and orphan's fund if we don't do something soon."

"Face it, Ben, she can't stand either one of us. We're going to have to figure out a way to get this place out of her hands and into ours."

"How do you suggest we do that? Maybe stick a letter opener in her back too?"

"We should be able to come up with something more original than that. Maybe cut the wires to the brakes in the limo."

"We could never get by Calvin. I think that guy sleeps with those cars. Maybe we could just push her down the stairs."

"There's no guarantee she'd die; she might just be paralyzed and then she'd stay in this place for the rest of her life and ours. We could drug her and shove her off a cliff."

"Lets think about it over drinks at the pub. All this talk about murder has made me thirsty."

*****

"I hope you like Italian food," said Fletch. "I have some Italian blood in me on my mother's side and have been craving some good old-fashioned Italian cooking."

"Like your mother used to make?"

"No, she's a terrible cook. I mean more like Armati's in Chicago. Benivitto's is almost as good."

Samantha could smell the wonderful aroma of garlic and spices before Fletch even opened the door for her. The restaurant was charming with its red and white checkered tablecloths and Chianti bottles holding candlesticks on the tables.

"It's nothing fancy," he said, "but the food is good and filling. I hope you're hungry."

"If I wasn't before, the smell of the Italian spices is making me hungry now. I've never heard of this place, not that I've been to many restaurants in town. I never had the time or money for much of a social life."

"I take it then there isn't anyone special in your life."

"If you mean a boyfriend, no there isn't. I had to study too hard and work through the first four years to be able to get my degree. Then this last year, I've spent most of my time at Stonehill Manor. I think the last date I had was two years ago and that didn't work out well at all."

"He wanted payment for the date?"

"He expected it and we'd gone Dutch. I don't know why he never asked me out again." Samantha laughed.

They ordered drinks and Samantha told him about the conversation she'd earlier with Daphne. How strange it was that Miss Schindler never answered Gretchen when she called to her and that her dinner was left untouched. Fletch told her about Officer Cummings and his theory that Ellen Schindler was asleep when the kidnapping took place.

"I did some checking into the professor's personnel records," said Samantha. "Miss Schindler wrote to him two years after the kidnapping apologizing for letting the baby be taken. The Professor apparently wrote to her saying she wasn't to blame. She wrote back thanking him for his understanding. The return address listed her name as Ellen Sawyer with an address in Wilmington. I looked up the address and it appears she's still living there."

"You really do make a good detective. I wouldn't mind paying a visit to Mrs. Sawyer. Would you like to come with me? Wilmington is only a couple of hours from here."

"Is it legal for me to come along on official police business?"

"Probably not, but this is unofficial and I'm just a concerned citizen looking for information. She doesn't have to say a word to me if she doesn't want to."

*****

Samantha enjoyed every bite of her fettuccine Alfredo. Although Hattie was an excellent cook, the meals served at Stonehill Manor were nothing like this.

Fletch smiled at her as she ate. He liked the fact that she was obviously enjoying her meal. He hadn't been out with too many women since arriving in Lancashire but the ones he'd dated usually left half of their meal on their plate fearing the extra calories.

She looked up at him watching her.

"What is it? Do I have sauce on my face?"

"No, I like watching you eat."

"I'm not very ladylike, am I? My dad always said I had a hollow leg. I can understand why you like this place; it's terrific."

Samantha liked the fact that he was watching her even though it didn't mean anything. Fletch was preoccupied with the professor's murder and didn't show any signs of being interested in her as a woman. She was kidding herself if she thought she had a chance with him. She imagined he had a string of gorgeous women trailing after him. Even their waitress tonight couldn't take her eyes off him. He did seem to like playing detective with her though and that was better than nothing.

The waitress stopped by their table with a tempting array of dessert offerings. They both declined the sweet-treats but did accept a cup of coffee.

"How are the frat boys? Are they still joined at the hip?" asked Fletch.

"You don't like them much, do you? I still think they're plotting to take Stonehill Manor away from me. Not that I blame them, you know. I think I'd feel the same way if the situation was reversed."

"Do you think you'll stay there when you're finished at the university?"

"I haven't decided yet. I'm sure the professor had something in mind when he left the mansion to me. Shutting it down would leave all the staff homeless and unemployed. I don't think I can do that to them after they have lived the better part of their lives there."

"Maybe you could charge the Pennington brothers rent. That would give the staff something to do."

"They would probably choose homelessness over waiting on those two. I couldn't do that to them. I did have a thought but it's probably a far-fetched idea."

"Maybe not; what were you thinking?"

"It's been on my mind since visiting the Melbourne School. That old building of theirs is in desperate need of repair in so many areas. With some renovation, Stonehill Manor might suit the students better. There certainly are enough bedrooms and space on the first floor for classrooms. The entire mansion is wheelchair accessible. Do you think it's a stupid idea?"

"It's a great idea. Have you mentioned this to anyone at the school?"

"No, I should talk to the professor's lawyer first. There are so many things that I would have to work through first. I don't know if I have a legal right to do it. Also, I'm not sure the director of the school would even consider moving so far away from their present site."

*****

While Fletch and Samantha enjoyed their meal, across town warming the bar stools at their favorite local pub, the Pennington brothers were on their third martini while scheming ways to eject Ms. Samantha Degan from Stonehill Manor and their lives.

"I can't understand why she isn't falling at my feet, Gil. That cop is getting her attention these days. He's blinding her to my charm."

"She's not blind to your charm, Ben; she's just not attracted to you. She likes a guy who takes charge. You've heard the servants talk about how the cop handcuffed her and hauled her off to jail; now she's sleeping with him. I know you thought you could get her to marry you so we could get our hands on Stonehill but that's going to take too long. We need to eliminate her."

"Are you kidding? You want to kill her?"

"Not me, you fool; we'll hire somebody to do the job. These pros can make it look like an accident."

"So she dies, then what? Did you hear anything about Stonehill falling back into our hands if Ms. Degan isn't around? Knowing dear old Uncle Fen, he probably left it to the servants. I wouldn't put it past him. He never treated them befitting of their station in life. I've got another idea, one that's less messy than murder. Do you remember Mother telling us how Uncle Fen bought jewelry for Aunt Veronica before she went loony?"

"Yes, I do remember, and Father said it was a waste to keep it locked up in a bedroom safe. Do you think it's still in the mansion?"

"I think it's not only in the mansion but in the safe in old Fen's bedroom. Don't you remember when we were kids that wall safe was right there behind that big painting? The door to his room is never locked. The servants don't like going in there because of the murder. Samantha's the only one I've ever seen sitting at his desk. We could wait until she goes off with the cop and try to open it."

"Then what, Ben? We take the jewelry and sell it? Uncle Fen was so meticulous; he probably has each piece listed somewhere. We might get caught."

"We take the jewelry, have fakes made, return the fakes to the safe and then go back home to sell the real stuff. Nobody is going to check the safe any time soon."

"I need to think about this over another martini, Ben. Bartender, two more of these and go easy on the olives. Too much salt isn't good for our health."

CHAPTER 13

The next morning, Samantha insisted she wanted to drive her VW that day.

"Calvin, I have many errands to take care of today and I don't want to monopolize your time. It's not that I don't appreciate your willingness to drive me anywhere I need to go, but I'd rather be on my own. I hope you understand."

"Yes, ma'am, I understand. I suppose I can be somewhat of a pest."

Samantha felt guilty putting him off, but she didn't want anyone to know she was seeing Fletch again today. They planned to drive to Wilmington to see what the Stonehill's former nanny had to say.

Samantha parked her car in the parking lot across the street from the police station. Her heart skipped a beat as she walked through the doors. The night she'd been brought here in handcuffs came back to her in that instant. She had been upset over the professor's death and mortified that the police thought she'd killed him. She gave the clerk at the front desk her name and was given a visitor's badge. Fletch met her in the hallway.

"You're right on time, Samantha," he said with a warm smile. "Come into my office. Robin found something interesting in the archived files."

"Good morning, Samantha. I understand you and my partner are doing some sleuthing this morning."

"So it would seem. I hope I'm not in the way. Will you be going with us?"

"No, I have desk duty today while I go through these old files. Show her the memo, Fletch."

"It's a memo to file from Chief Clayton. He personally investigated the Stonehill kidnapping. I'll let you read it, but it doesn't sound promising that we will ever find out what happened to the baby."

Samantha read through the memo until she got to the last paragraph:

.... After an exhaustive investigation and without concrete evidence, I must conclude the kidnapping of Amari Joy Stonehill was executed by a professional for the sole purpose of human trafficking....

Samantha thought she was going to be sick to her stomach.

"Who would do such a thing? Poor Professor Stonehill; he had to live with the fear that his daughter was sold into slavery."

"It's sickening what humans can do to others for money," said Robin. She was more hardened to the atrocities of life than Samantha, but it was still difficult for her to comprehend the cruelty in the world.

"I'm sorry, Samantha, I probably shouldn't have shown that to you. Chief Clayton retired within weeks after he closed the case. He's still living in Lancashire. I'm going to be talking to him as soon as I can arrange a time. First, we'll see what the nanny has to offer. Are you ready to go?"

"I think so. I'm sorry to be such a wimp, but I never imagined something so terrible could have happened to that baby. I can't imagine what thoughts went through the professor's mind all these years. No wonder his poor wife escaped into her own world."

*****

On the two-hour drive to Wilmington, Samantha couldn't get the images of children in slavery out of her mind. She and Fletch barely spoke during the ride. He knew she was processing the information she'd read and understood her need to be silent and think. He'd been in that place himself when he started on the force in Chicago.

When they arrived in Wilmington, it didn't take long for Fletch to find the address Samantha had located for Mrs. Ellen Sawyer.

It was a pretty older home on a tree-lined street. The house reminded Samantha of the home where she'd grown up. There were flowers in window boxes and in pots on the front porch. It was very inviting.

"Here we are," said Fletch. "Are you sure you want to be a part of this?"

"Yes, now more than ever. I want to know who the monster was who stole the professor's baby."

*****

An attractive woman in her early forties answered the door. Samantha could hear soft music playing in the background. Other than that, it was quiet.

"Hello, Mrs. Sawyer. My name is Detective Joe Fletcher from the Lancashire Police Department and this is Samantha Degan. We would like to ask you some questions about a kidnapping that took place some twenty years ago."

Mrs. Sawyer's face turned white. She didn't say anything for what seemed an eternity.

Fletch didn't push her; he just silently waited for a response.

"Have they found the baby?" she asked.

"I'm afraid not. Would you be willing to talk with us about her disappearance?"

"Yes, I'll talk with you. I'll never forgive myself for the part I played in that beautiful baby's kidnapping.

I'm afraid I wasn't much help back then. I lied to the police at the time and have never gotten over the guilt."

"You lied to the police? What did you lie about?"

"Can I get you some coffee? Please come in; I have some cookies in the oven. I like to have something sweet for the children when they come home from school."

Fletch followed Samantha into the attractively decorated living room. There were children's pictures covering the mantle.

"Those are my children, the youngest is just five and is in kindergarten this year. I find I don't know what to do with myself when they're all in school. Ross, that's my husband, doesn't want me to get a job. He thinks it's best I stay home with the children. I'm not sure what kind of job I'd qualify for. The only thing I know is taking care of kids and nobody would ever hire me after what happened to little Mari."

"Would you like to talk about Mari and what happened that day?"

Fletch was being patient with the woman; he sensed she was finding it difficult to talk about the kidnapping and wanted her to feel at ease.

"I did the worst thing a nanny can do," she offered. "I left the baby alone while I had a rendezvous with a young man. I told everyone I turned my back to warm Mari's bottle but in reality, I was meeting a boy in the rose garden." She began to sob. Samantha sat next to her and put her hand on her shoulder. Finally, Mrs. Sawyer composed herself and continued, "I have never told anyone the truth about what happened that night. I was so ashamed. I met Arthur in the park when I'd taken Mari there in her carriage once. It's only about a mile from Stonehill Manor and it was a beautiful spring day. I loved the walk and I'd done it often when the weather was nice. I was sitting on a park bench when

Arthur Bennett sat down next to me and introduced himself. He was so handsome and I felt comfortable with him immediately. He told me he was going to the university. He said I was prettier than any of the girls in the school. He walked me back to the mansion and asked me to meet him at seven o'clock in the rose garden behind the mansion. I told him I couldn't leave the baby, but he said she wouldn't know I was gone if she was sleeping.

"As it turned out, Mari was asleep at seven. I walked down the back stairs where nobody would see me and out to the garden. He was there and I let him kiss me. At first, he was gentle and sweet and then he started kissing me harder and groping me. I told him to stop but he kept on until I cried that he was hurting me. He asked me why I'd met him if I wasn't going to have some fun. I managed to break away and I ran back into the mansion.

"I saw the tray Gretchen had left for me but I couldn't think about food. I was so ashamed of my behavior and what had almost happened out there in the rose garden. I looked in on Mari but she was gone. I don't remember much after that. I know I was taken to the hospital, but I never told the doctors or therapists what I'd done."

"You don't remember seeing anyone going in or coming out of the mansion? Maybe they knew about the back stairs that were out of sight of the rest of the staff."

"I'm sure I didn't see anyone. Those stairs are hidden from the rose garden. I suppose whoever took the baby could have slipped out that way and I wouldn't have seen them even if I was looking."

Her face turned scarlet at the thought of what she was doing at the moment the baby was stolen.

"If only I had been with Mari instead of out there with that horrible boy, she wouldn't have been taken."

"That's not necessarily true. If the kidnapper was after the baby, he wouldn't have let you get in the way. You might have been hurt or even killed and then these five beautiful children wouldn't have been born," Fletch said as he glanced at the mantle.

*****

On the drive back to Lancashire, Fletch called Robin on his cell phone.

"How'd it go partner?" she asked when she recognized his number.

"It turns out the nanny was with some guy in the rose garden when the baby turned up missing. The kid's name was Arthur Bennett and he claimed he was enrolled in the university at the time of the kidnapping."

"You want me to check him out? I'll get right on it and call you back."

Not five minutes later, Fletch's cell phone rang.

"That was quick."

"Our friend wasn't that hard to find. He flunked out of the university before the second semester even began. He now manages that fancy health spa at the corner of Fourth and Lincoln right here in our fair city."

"Thanks, Robin. I think Sam and I will pay him a visit when we get back to town."

He looked over at Samantha and she nodded in agreement.

*****

The spa was indeed upscale. Samantha had driven by it many times on her way to her job at the drug store during her sophomore year. She knew without inquiring that she wouldn't be able to afford the membership fee. At least now, she'd see if it was as luxurious as she'd imagined all these years.

It was late afternoon when Fletch pulled into the parking lot next to the building. There were several cars in the lot, most were late-model, high-priced vehicles.

Fletch opened the door to the building for Samantha and she almost gasped. It was more beautiful inside than she'd ever imagined. She felt as though she had stepped on a movie set with the velvet upholstered furniture and a chandelier that took up most of the ceiling space in the lobby. Leather-paneled counters were at the far end with clerks that could easily pass for models standing behind them.

"Welcome to Serenity Spa and Fitness Center; how may I help you?" said the gorgeous blonde as the equally gorgeous brunette eyed Fletch.

"I'm Detective Joe Fletcher and this is Samantha Degan. We are here to speak with Arthur Bennett if he's available."

There was a flicker of alarm on the blonde's face while the brunette turned her attention back to the magazine she was reading.

"I'll see if Mr. Bennett is in," the blonde said with a slight quiver in her voice. "Art, there are a couple of cops here to see you," she whispered into the phone receiver.

*****

Within seconds, a man of around forty-five with a deep tan and a shirt unbuttoned to the middle of his chest appeared.

"I'm Art Bennett, Officer. How may I be of service to you? There's no trouble with the spa, I hope."

"No, Mr. Bennett, we're here to ask you some questions about the evening the daughter of Professor and Mrs. Fenwick Stonehill was kidnapped. We understand you were with Miss Ellen Schindler on the property of Stonehill Manor at the time."

"Hey, you're not pinning that kidnapping on me. I didn't have anything to do with it. Besides, it happened a long time ago, why are you asking about it now?"

"Perhaps you'd like to move this conversation to the privacy of your office?"

"Yes, please, come with me but I'm innocent. Isn't there a statute of limitation or something like that?"

"There is no limitation relevant to the crime of kidnapping. We are here to gather information. You are under no obligation to speak to me."

"Listen, I had nothing to do with that kidnapping. I was meeting the kid's nanny. I don't remember her name, but she was hot to trot if you get my meaning." He looked at Samantha and seemed to see her for the first time. "You don't look like a cop; you're much too beautiful. No offense, Officer Fletcher, it's just that the lady is more my style than you are." He laughed at his own little joke.

"No offense taken. Now back to the night of the kidnapping, did you see or hear anything that caused you alarm?"

"Not a thing. I can't say I was paying much attention. I saw the nanny in the park earlier in the day. She was kind of prim and proper but there was something about her that made me think I wanted to get a piece of that. You know what I mean." He winked at Fletch.

"No, I can't say that I do; go on."

"I sat down next to her and she got all flustered. It didn't take long before she softened up. I offered to walk her home and she jumped at the chance. I couldn't believe it when I saw the place she was living in. I'd heard of Professor Stonehill—everybody at the university knew who he was. I knew the guy was rich but I had no idea how rich until I saw that mansion. By then, the little nanny was so gaga over me, she couldn't see straight. I thought I'd give her a thrill and offer to meet her later that night. I figured we'd end up in the kid's room eventually. It turned out she was a dud after all. She ran away before we got to the good stuff." His laugh gave Samantha the creeps.

"Thank you, Mr. Bennett. I think that's all for now. I'll let you know if I have any more questions for you."

"Anytime, Officer. Please feel free to stop by again and bring the little lady with you. We know how to treat women around here."

*****

"He's slime, but I don't think he can help us with the case."

"He made my skin crawl. I feel the need to take a shower after that encounter."

"He was leering at you, wasn't he? I can't imagine a woman like Ellen Schindler Sawyer falling for a jerk like that."

"Maybe he was more appealing twenty years ago. I'm glad she was able to fight him off. I doubt she would have survived the ordeal if things had gone further than they did."

"I didn't realize it was getting so late. Are they are expecting you back at the mansion?"

"I told Daphne I might not be home in time for dinner. I think she suspects I'm with you but she won't say anything to the others. She doesn't want them gossiping about me or anyone else. Daphne is like a mother hen with her chicks, even though they're all pushing sixty and seventy."

"It's like a family, isn't it?"

"Very much so. They all loved the professor and each other. It worries me because I can't go on being the mistress of the manor forever and I don't know what will become of them then."

"I was under the impression the professor provided for them in his will. They should all be eligible, or nearly eligible, for Social Security. Between the inheritance and their benefits, wouldn't that be enough for them to live on?"

"It probably would be but they wouldn't be together and that's what keeps them going. I can't imagine either Millie or Betsy living on their own. I doubt either one of them even has a checkbook. Right or wrong, they've been protected by Daphne and George since they came to live and work at Stonehill Manor."

"You're a really good person, Samantha Degan. I don't know how I could have suspected you of murder."

Fletch was trying his best to deny his attraction to Samantha. He didn't need to complicate his life now and, besides, she was way out of his league. Whether she felt comfortable with it or not, she was indeed mistress of Stonehill Manor and that meant she was wealthy. He knew that she would adjust to her position eventually and when she did, a lowly cop would be beneath her. Robin had told him more than once that he needed a social life. It was true; he hadn't dated much since arriving in Lancashire. There was the waitress at Barney's; she wasn't bad-looking but she never stopped talking. Karen, who worked in the travel agency was pretty but all she talked about was her ex and how much she despised him. There were others but he couldn't recall their names. He liked being a bachelor with nobody telling him what to do. There were times, though, when he was lonely but fortunately, those times didn't happen too often.

*****

"You're lost in thought," said Samantha.

"Sorry, you're right. I was thinking about the case," he lied. "Tell me about yourself, what was your life like before you started working for the professor."

"I don't think anyone has ever asked me that before. I'll have to admit, I'm pretty boring. As I told you, I'm the youngest of five children and the only girl. My brothers treated me like a porcelain doll. They intimidated any boy who showed up at our front door, so, I didn't date much," she laughed.

"You would be worth a bloody nose," said Fletch.

"Detective Fletcher, that's the nicest thing you have ever said to me."

"I'd better watch it or you will find out I'm not such a bad guy after all."

CHAPTER 14

"Ben, get up. Samantha has been out of the house all morning. Let's go open the safe in Uncle's room."

"Gilford, you do it; I've got a headache. I need more sleep."

"Bentley, you drink too much. Now get up and take a couple of aspirin. We've got work to do while Samantha's out. The sooner we get into that safe and pawn the jewelry, the sooner we'll be able to get out of this cruddy town."

"I thought you were going to have fakes made to replace it."

"No. I got to thinking, nobody knows the jewelry is still around. Aunt Veronica was off her rocker years ago and never wore it again. Uncle Fenwick is dead so he's not going to look for the stuff. We'll just take it all and keep it ourselves."

"I feel better already. That little twit has stolen everything else from us. Let's take what belongs to us."

Gilford checked the hallway of the third floor. The Professor's suite was dusted every day at precisely eight o'clock, which meant the maids had come and gone. The brothers had complete privacy on this floor at this time of day.

"I know how to break into a safe, Gil. I've seen them do it in the movies and it's easy." They quickly ran into the professor's room, shut the door, and headed for the safe.

Bentley turned the dial around and around with his ear against it, waiting for the noise of the tumblers to fall into place.

"Get out of the way, Ben. You don't know what you're doing. Let me try. Uncle Fen didn't have much imagination, I'll bet he used something obvious like Mother's birthday."

Gil turned the dial to the numbers of the date of his mother's birth and then cranked the handle. The safe door opened. He reached in and pulled out a large box. When he lifted the lid—sure enough—there were necklaces and bracelets and earrings, all sparkling with diamonds and other precious gems.

"We did it, Ben! Look at this stuff. It will be worth a fortune." He started to close the door to the safe.

"No, wait Gil; let's see what else is in there." Ben reached in and pulled out a stack of letters. "Look, I'd recognize Mother's handwriting anywhere. I wonder why she wrote letters to Uncle Fen instead of just calling him."

"People wrote letters back in those days. Now put them back and let's get out of here."

"No, I want to read them." Ben reached into the safe again and pulled out a photo album. "Look, Gil, these are pictures of Aunt Veronica. She was a real looker; old Uncle Fen was a lucky man."

"Will you put that junk back? We're going to get caught if we don't get out of here now. Samantha could be back at any moment."

"Okay, but I'm taking the letters. I want to see what Mother wrote about. I'll put the album back because I'm sure it just has pictures of his dead wife."

"Let's go pack our things. I'll call Alice at Pennington's and have her send the jet to the airport. I don't want to pawn this stuff here in Lancashire; it might arouse suspicion so soon after Fen's murder."

The brothers went to their rooms where Gilford made the call in privacy and began packing. Bentley sat on the bed to read his mother's letters to her brother.

> *....Fen, I'm so worried about Bentley; he simply doesn't have any ambition.....Fen, please help me with Gilford; he says he's quitting school....Fen, I agree with what you say, I've spoiled the boys, but they're good children deep down....Fen, Bentley was expelled from Williamson for drinking alcohol in the boy's locker room....Fen, I can't handle the boys any longer; will you take them in, please?....Fen, I can't believe you aren't willing to help me with the boys; I thought you cared for me.....Fen, your last letter informed me you are refusing to leave Stonehill Manor to the boys in the event of your death. I will never forgive you for this.....Fen, I hope you've changed your mind about excluding the boys from your will.....I will fight you for their rightful inheritance, dear brother......*

That was the last of the letters. Bentley couldn't understand why Uncle Fenwick went against his mother's wishes. She had wanted her sons to have Stonehill Manor, but instead, the mansion was left to a stranger. For the first time in his life, he felt ashamed. He was sure it was the first time his uncle had refused Eliza anything and it all was because he and Gilford had made such a mess of their lives. He gathered the letters and placed them in his suitcase.

*****

Without fanfare, the brothers left the mansion and Calvin drove them to the airport. It was a relief to all the staff when Calvin returned to say he'd watched from the road as the Pennington jet took off and disappeared into the clouds.

Daphne couldn't wait for Samantha to arrive home to tell her the good news that the boys were gone.

*****

Fletch sat at his desk, leafing through the files on the kidnapping case. His instincts told him the two crimes were related. Had the professor uncovered information about the kidnapping? Had he confronted the person and needed to be silenced? The telephone on his desk rang.

"Detective Fletcher," he answered.

"Good evening, Detective; this is Paul Clayton. I understand you are assigned to Professor Stonehill's murder case."

"That's correct, Chief Clayton, and I know you handled the kidnapping of his daughter."

"Not very well, I'm afraid. We never solved the crime or—more importantly—we were never able to return the baby to her parents. I wonder if you would be willing to come to my home to talk about both cases. I'm afraid I don't get around too well anymore."

"I'd be happy to meet with you. In fact, I'm studying the kidnapping case as we speak. Your investigation was extremely thorough from what I can tell."

Chief Clayton gave Fletch his address. It was in the older part of town.

"I'll leave right away, Chief. I'll be there in fifteen minutes or so."

*****

Fletch drove to a well-kept tree-lined street. The Chief's home was the third house on the left. It was a white colonial with black shutters framing the windows. He walked up to a dark red door that looked like it had been freshly painted and rang the bell. An attractive older woman greeted him.

"You must be Detective Fletcher. I'm Susan Clayton. Please come in. My husband is expecting you."

A white-haired gentleman appeared in the doorway, walking slowly with the aid of a cane.

"Detective Fletcher, it's good to meet you, I'm Paul Clayton."

"It's a pleasure, sir. I've heard many good things about you and your leadership."

"I enjoyed the job, even though Lancashire isn't exactly the crime capital of the country," he laughed. "Come sit in the library. I'm anxious to hear what you have to say about Fen's murder."

"I'm afraid there isn't much to tell. Who killed him and why is still a mystery. He doesn't seem to have had an enemy in the world. My partner and I are going over the files on the kidnapping case, looking for something that links the two crimes."

"I know the frustration you feel. I felt it years ago. I knew Fenwick Stonehill and his wife socially. That was the reason I took over the case. I foolishly thought I would be the one to bring their baby back home to them. To this day, I'm convinced it was a professional job and that baby was sold to the highest bidder. I couldn't forgive myself for not being able to solve the case."

"I understand your frustration, sir. I'm beginning to feel the same way about the professor's murder."

"What about the young woman who was hired to help him write his memoirs? I understand she found his body."

"Yes, she not only found the body, she was seen holding the murder weapon in her hand. The coroner's report cleared her of any wrongdoing. I've gotten to know Samantha Degan and I'm convinced she did not commit the crime."

The chief smiled. "You wouldn't be the first cop to fall for a suspect in a crime."

"Oh no, sir. I don't have feelings for Samantha; she's simply helping me with some details of the case. There isn't anything more to our relationship than that."

"Whatever you say, Detective. I might be an old man but I could see your eyes light up at the mention of her name."

Fletch thought it best to drop the subject but it did make him uncomfortable. He and Paul Clayton discussed the kidnapping case and the murder for the next two hours. Mrs. Clayton knocked on the door after the first hour.

"I don't want to disturb you, but it's time for Paul's brandy. I thought you might like to join him."

"That's very nice of you, Mrs. Clayton," Fletch said as he reached for the glasses placing one in front of the Chief.

"My wife thinks the brandy makes me sleep better. I'm not sure if it does, but I do like her way of thinking."

Fletch left the Clayton home with a better understanding of why the old timers at the station had such admiration for their former boss. He couldn't forgive himself for his failure to solve the Stonehill kidnapping case and had resigned his position on the force the day he officially closed the case. Fletch was now even more determined to uncover the mystery of both crimes.

He thought of the nurse who'd worked the night shift tending to the professor. Robin had interviewed her but had found nothing to show she had anything to do with the murder. Tomorrow he would talk to her again. She was the last person, other than the murderer, to see the professor alive. Maybe she had more information than she realized.

He began to think about what the Chief had said about Samantha. The old man didn't know what he was talking about. He said his eyes lit up at the mention of her name. That was the most ridiculous thing he'd ever heard. Sure, she was beautiful and smart and made him laugh. She had a way with kids too. He'd liked the way she acted with the children when they visited the Melbourne School. They took an instant liking to her and you can't fool kids. He'd also liked the idea that she was thinking of giving Stonehill Manor to the school. She said the only thing, other than the staff, she'd miss about the mansion was her big overstuffed bed. The more he thought about it, the more he wondered if there was some truth to what the Chief said.

CHAPTER 15

Daphne opened the door for Samantha when she saw her walking toward the kitchen from the garage area.

"You won't believe it. The Pennington brothers packed their bags and left this afternoon. Calvin watched as the Pennington jet took off from the airport with the boys definitely on it."

"That was sudden. Have you counted the silver?" Samantha chuckled.

"No, but maybe I will," Daphne answered in all seriousness.

"I'm glad they're out of here, but I doubt we've seen the last of them. They won't rest until they're able to gain control of Stonehill Manor. Oh, Daphne, life was so much simpler when I was living in a crowded dorm at the university."

"I'm glad they're gone too. They made all of us feel uncomfortable. They thought we were mere servants. I realize that's what we are, but the professor never treated us that way and neither do you. How was your day with Detective Fletcher?"

"He interviewed Amari's nanny. She has a family of her own now. Fletch thinks the kidnapping and the professor's murder are related. As much as I'd like the killer found, I'm not sure I want to be involved in the investigation."

"You're in love with the detective, aren't you?"

"Is it that obvious? He doesn't think of me in that way. Once his case is solved, he'll forget all about me."

"He has a partner, doesn't he?"

"Yes."

"Have you wondered why he's dragging you into this investigation when it makes more sense for him to rely on his partner to help him?"

"Robin is busy going over the kidnapping case files. I was the one who found the married name and address of the former Miss Schindler and that's why he asked me to go along with him today."

"Nonsense; he asked you to go along with him because he wanted your company. It's obvious the two of you are attracted to each other."

Samantha was relieved when the uncomfortable conversation was interrupted by the ringing of her cell phone.

"Where have you been? I was worried about you. I called a couple of times and you didn't answer. There's a murderer out there somewhere, you know."

"I'm sorry you worried, Detective," she said in surprise. "I decided to get some research done at the library on the way home from the station and turned my phone off while I was there. I just got home and haven't checked my messages."

"I guess I was letting my imagination get the better of me. I had a visit with Chief Clayton this evening. He hasn't forgiven himself for not finding the baby years ago. I didn't get anything new from him except a determination to find her if she is still alive. What do you know about the nurse who left him alone the day of the murder? I know Robin talked to her but she didn't have any useful information. I think I'll talk to her again tomorrow. Would you like to go with me?"

"Yes I would; is it another unofficial visit?"

"Yes, but don't tell my boss," he whispered.

*****

"I didn't mean to eavesdrop," said Daphne after Samantha had put away her cellphone, "but I'm assuming the handsome detective has requested your presence once again in his investigation?"

"Yes, but don't read anything into it. He's just doing his job."

Daphne smiled when she saw the color rise in Samantha's cheeks.

*****

The next morning, Fletch arrived at the mansion at eight o'clock sharp. Judy Pryor had agreed to meet with him and Samantha after her overnight shift ended.

"I didn't tell you that the Pennington brothers left for home yesterday. I think I've seen the last of them unless they decide to take me to court to fight the professor's will."

"They left? Did you count the silver?"

"That's exactly what I asked Daphne."

"It's suspicious that they would give up so easily. They must have another plan in their devious minds. Either that or they robbed you blind before they left."

"Maybe Daphne should count the silver after all."

*****

They arrived at Judy Pryor's house just as she was pulling into the driveway.

"I'm glad I didn't miss you. I was unavoidably delayed waiting for Mrs. Handley's day nurse to arrive. Despite what you might think, Samantha, I don't always leave my patients unattended."

"I'm sure you don't, Judy. I believe you said you had a sick child at home. I only wish you'd called me before you left the professor to fend for himself."

"I know I should have and look what happened. I gave whoever killed him ample time to do the deed and I feel really guilty about that."

"Ms. Pryor, we aren't here to judge your actions, only to ask a few questions about that evening. Did you notice anything unusual that night? Did you hear noises in the hallway that would indicate someone was near the professor's room? Was there a window left open? Anything at all that got your attention?"

"There is something that has been gnawing at me. I'd forgotten about it until a few nights ago when something happened to trigger my memory. My patient's maid knocked on Mrs. Handley's door around five o'clock in the morning. She handed me an envelope and said Mrs. Handley's attorney had sent it over for her signature the night before. Mrs. Handley is always awake by that time. Anyway, it made me remember the last night I was at Stonehill Manor. I'd gone to the kitchen to make myself a cup of tea. When I passed by the front door on my way back upstairs, I heard a soft knock. It was close to ten o'clock and the servants were all in their rooms for the night. Samantha, I think you had gone to the university library."

Samantha nodded in agreement and remembered she'd been at the library until closing time.

"I opened the door and there was a young man standing there with a large envelope in his hand. He said he had instructions to give the envelope to Professor Stonehill personally. I told him the professor was asleep and that I'd give it to him when he woke up. He said he was only following orders and he hoped he wouldn't get in trouble. I told him I wouldn't tell his boss and he seemed satisfied. I took the envelope and put it on the professor's desk so he wouldn't miss it in the morning. Because I was worried about my own daughter, I forgot all about it. I'm sure the professor saw it because I helped him from his bed to the wheelchair and wheeled him to his desk just before I left. He couldn't have missed it."

"Was it a manila envelope?" Fletch asked.

"Yes, in fact, it was. Did I do the right thing? I didn't open it. I didn't think anything could be so important that it couldn't wait until morning."

"You did the right thing, Judy," Samantha assured her. "The professor always benefited from a good night's sleep."

"Do you remember how thick the envelope was? Was it sealed? Did it have a return address?"

"I remember thinking it must have been some kind of report. If something that size was to be mailed, it would need two or maybe three postage stamps. It was sealed and I don't believe there was a return address. The Professor's name was scrawled on the outside and the lettering was very bold. My guess is that it was a man's handwriting. It also had the word CONFIDENTIAL printed in the left-hand corner. I'm sorry I never told the policewoman who questioned me about the envelope. I didn't think about it until now. Is it helpful at all?"

"It could be. Is there anything else you can think of about that night? Did the delivery boy drive a car?"

"I don't remember seeing a car—oh wait—he was on a bicycle. I watched him from the window and worried that he could easily be hit on the highway. It was a very dark and cloudy night and the moon was barely visible."

"Was there anything unusual about the delivery boy? Was he young? Maybe a student at the university?"

"Yes, he was young and, yes, he probably was a student. He didn't wait for a tip and I remember thinking that was strange. My purse was in the professor's room and I told him to wait while I went to get it but he said, no, he didn't want to wait. I had the feeling he wanted to get out of there as soon as he could."

Fletch gave Judy his card and asked her to call his cell phone if she thought of anything else. She agreed and again apologized for leaving the professor alone that fateful night.

"A manila envelope was delivered hours before the professor was murdered. You found a torn corner of a manila envelope in his desk drawer. I would love to know what was inside."

"You're thinking he hired a private detective, aren't you?"

"That's what it sounds like to me. It's not unusual for one to hire some kid to deliver their findings. They don't like to be identified by the person who accepts delivery if it's someone other than their client. It's obvious the professor wasn't able to meet the guy on a street corner to collect a report. Now we have to figure out who he was having investigated and why."

CHAPTER 16

"Bentley, will you stop reading those stupid letters. So what if Uncle Fenwick didn't approve of the way we live, we have his wife's jewelry and we'll have fun spending the money we get from it."

"Our poor mother practically begged the old goat to help her out with us. I think he left our family's estate to Samantha just for spite. We were always charming when we were around him. I can't believe he turned on us."

"Ben, you fool, the last time we visited Uncle Fenwick was when we were in prep school. He was a pain in the neck then. Don't you remember he kept telling us we had to shape up? We vowed not to visit him again until after he was dead. We kept that promise," Gilford snickered. "Let's get the jewelry and get to the pawn shop. Willard Humphrey says this guy, Percy, is a pushover. We're going to get top dollar for the loot."

"I hope so. Alfred Nottingham is getting stingy about our allowance. He's forgotten whose name is on the corporate letterhead."

*****

The pawn shop was on the west side of town. The brothers rode together in Gilford's car. Bentley was too nervous to drive in the area.

"I don't like it here, Gil. What if we run out of gas or have a flat tire? There are a lot of murders in this part of town."

"You're just like a little old woman, Bentley. You worry too much, you know that." If the truth be known, Gil wasn't feeling as confident as he pretended.

"There it is, Percy's Pawn Shop. With a name like that, I can't believe the guy's able to do business down here."

The brothers walked into the shop. Gilford held the box of jewelry tightly under his arm. He'd appointed himself as spokesman for the duo.

"What can I do for you, boys?" a voice boomed.

"We're looking for Percy,"

"Well, you found him. Whatcha got there? Must be something good the way you're holding it."

It was dark in the store and the closer they got to the counter where Percy was standing, the larger he looked. Gilford had to raise his head to look Percy in the eye.

He found his voice and lied that they had some of their dearly departed mother's jewelry they thought would interest the pawn shop owner.

"Come closer, boys. I'm not going to hurt you," he snarled. "Not yet anyway. Let's see what you have here."

Gilford opened the box and gingerly took each piece out, laying it gently on the counter.

Bentley's heart was beating so fast; he was sure the big oaf could hear it. He could feel the perspiration running down the back of his neck. Percy looked down at him and sneered; he was enjoying watching these rich dudes shaking in their designer shoes.

Percy reached into a drawer under the counter and pulled out a jeweler's hand-held loupe to examine the gems. He shone a bright light on each one, turning them over again and again. It was silent in the shop except for the tick-tock of the clock on the wall. Bentley noticed his heart was beating in rhythm to the sounds of the clock.

After what seemed an eternity, Percy frowned at the brothers.

"Are you trying to swindle Percy?" he shouted. "Fakes, they're all fakes. Now, get out of my shop and take this junk with you."

The boys quickly gathered the jewelry and ran to the door, dropping a few pieces on the floor as they left.

Percy watched their hasty departure from the window. This wasn't going to be a total loss. He could sell the bracelet and ring that those idiots had dropped on their way out of the store. But he wasn't about to take on any of that other stuff. He might have gotten some big bucks for some of that junk but he had to be careful what he carried. The cops were always watching him to make sure his business was legit.

*****

"Fakes, they're all fakes! How could Uncle do this to us, Gil? We could have been killed in there. That guy was an Amazon."

"Shut up and let me think."

Bentley knew better than to interrupt his brother when he was trying to solve a dilemma. He sat quietly, looking out the window at the crumbling houses and apartment buildings nearby. He had no sympathy for people who chose to live in poverty like this. They simply had no ambition to better themselves.

"Bentley, we're fools. Of course, that stuff was fake. Mother never wore her gems in public. They were locked up in a safe-deposit box at the bank for safe keeping. She wore the fakes and I'll bet her friends all did the same. They were always afraid of the good stuff being stolen right off their necks. Do you remember seeing a key in Fenwick's safe?"

"I don't know, Gil; I wasn't looking for a key."

"No, you were too engrossed in those stupid letters. Why do I have to do everything myself? You really are worthless. We'll have to go back to Stonehill Manor and find that key."

"What makes you think the bank will turn over the contents of the box without calling Uncle's lawyer?"

"You have a point. We'll have to figure another way to get what's rightfully ours. We'll have to take Samantha to court."

*****

The day only got worse for the brothers. As they pulled into the driveway of the Pennington estate, they recognized Edward Andersen's Lexus parked in front of the mansion. Edward was their father's lawyer and had continued to represent the family and the corporation after his death. He never had much time or regard for the Pennington brothers. He thought they were useless playboys and nothing like their father.

"Edward, to what do we owe this unexpected visit?" asked Bentley.

"Come into your father's study, boys. I have some business I need to discuss with you."

Bentley poured Gil and himself a drink and sat down on the overstuffed leather chair. Edward sat at the desk and opened his briefcase.

"There's no other way to say this except to just say it. Clarence Pope, Pennington's CEO and Jackson Elliot, the CFO have been embezzling funds from your father's company since his death. They apparently set up accounts in Switzerland and have both disappeared. Boys, I'm afraid Pennington's is broke and so are you. Your stock in the company is worthless."

"That can't be," said Bentley in a whisper. "Our family is worth billions; it can't be gone."

"I've warned you boys since your father died that you had to take an interest in the company or you would lose everything one day. You both were more interested in being carefree playboys and now that day has come."

"What about the mansion? Surely we'll be able to keep it?" said Gilford.

"You can probably hold on to it for another few months, but the cost of running this place and paying the servants is astronomical. As your lawyer, I recommend you sell it. You both will be able to continue your lifestyle for a few years with the profits. Don't you share an apartment in the city?"

"Yes, but this is our home. We've lived here since we were born. You can't expect us to give it up."

"I don't like to see it go. It's one of the landmarks in the south. Your folks had some fabulous parties in this old place. However, because of your financial situation, you will not be able to support it or the staff."

"What are we going to do, Gilford? We're paupers."

"Have you boys ever thought of getting jobs? I know you have good educations. Maybe it's time you got out there and worked for a living."

"Just what are you suggesting, Edward? That Bentley and I become used car salesmen? Seriously, who would hire two men in their thirties who've never worked a day in their lives? We're doomed."

"You could always marry into a wealthy family. I know Pamela Enright has always been smitten with you, Bentley. Her daddy comes from old money and she's a lawyer now. You might want to give her a call."

"Pamela Enright? That tall skinny kid with the braces on her teeth and thick glasses? I'd rather work for a living than marry her."

"She's grown into her height and her teeth look straight to me. I think the thick glasses are gone too. How long has it been since you've been to the monthly cocktail parties at the club? That's a good place to make contact with Pamela. She and some of the other women set up these parties. There's one tonight and I'm planning to stop by. You can ride with me. I'm sure you won't have any trouble finding a ride home."

"Are the drinks on you, Edward?"

"The first two are, after that you're on your own."

"We might as well go, Gil, we have nothing better to do. I can't make any promises about the Enright girl but I'll keep an open mind."

It had been a while since the boys had been to the country club. It was a place for their parent's age group to socialize. Tonight, the crowd looked younger than they remembered. Many looked like they'd just come in from playing a round of golf or finishing a tennis match. There were some faces they recognized but the tall willowy young woman who approached them didn't look familiar at all.

"Bentley Pennington, I can't believe it's you. It's been years since we last met."

"Good to see you again," he said, wondering how he could forget this beauty.

"You don't remember me, do you? I'm Pamela Enright. I used to have a tremendous crush on you. I'm afraid I made a terrible fool of myself back then."

"You're Pamela Enright? I'm sorry I didn't recognize you."

"Yes, I was an awkward teen. You always dated the petite girls. I wasn't your type at all but it didn't stop me from trying to get your attention," she laughed.

"You have my attention now," he said as he took her elbow and guided her to a table in the corner of the room.

CHAPTER 17

"How are you coming on the Stonehill investigation, partner? I think I've been replaced by the lovely Samantha."

"Nobody could replace you, Robin. I just thought the nurse might open up more if someone she knew was there while I asked my questions."

"Hey, I'm happy to see you enjoying the company of a female who meets my approval. The kids have asked about you. You haven't been to dinner since the Stonehill murder. Why don't you and Samantha come over tonight? Frank is making his famous enchiladas and there's always enough to feed an army."

"That does sound tempting, but I don't think Samantha would be interested in spending a social evening with me."

"Why do you say that? Anybody can see how you two look at each other. You're crazy about her, Detective, and my guess is she feels the same way about you. Call her and ask her about tonight or would you rather I called her?"

"I am perfectly capable of making my own dates, Robin. I'm just not sure she will accept. After all, she's a little too rich for my blood."

"Fletch, you are a fool. The girl doesn't come from money and I get the feeling she isn't comfortable having it now. She told me she'd like to find the professor's daughter so she can turn over the mansion and everything in it to her. What have you got against rich people anyway?"

"I have nothing against rich people; I just don't fit in with that crowd. How many socially elite cops do you know?"

"You're impossible; I give up."

Fletch smiled at her. He had managed to stop her matchmaking talk but did he really want her to stop?

"You're looking good these days, Robin. Frank must be doing the cooking."

"As a matter of fact, he is. I haven't had a particularly good relationship with food lately."

"What's wrong? Are you sick?"

"Fletch, for a detective, you are the most clueless man I know. I've had morning sickness for the last three months. Why do you think I've hung around the station? I don't like to get too far away from the can if you must know."

"You and Frank are going to have another kid? That's great news, Robin. I wondered why you didn't object when I took Samantha with me when I talked to witnesses."

"That's one reason and also because I think you two make a good team."

"You're not going to let up, are you? Let's talk about the case. I'm missing something important but I can't figure out what. I can't see any of the servants killing their boss; they seem to have worshipped the man. Their lives revolved completely around him and that mansion, and there's no sign that any of them were stealing from him. You did background checks on all of them and they're all squeaky clean."

"All except the chauffeur," said Robin. "He was in trouble as a teenager but nothing since then. He's been at the mansion for the shortest time, only about twenty years."

"The professor must have been quite a guy to have such loyal employees all these years. He didn't leave any of them out of his will, so he must have been on good terms with them all."

"But, I can't get over the idea that his killing and the baby's kidnapping are somehow related. I think the answer lies in the papers delivered on the night of the murder if only there was a way to find out what was in them."

"While you're thinking, make that call to Samantha. You need to get your mind off the case for an evening. You can continue your sleuthing tomorrow."

*****

Samantha was engrossed in her writing and didn't hear her cell phone ring. The first draft of Professor Stonehill's memoirs was finally completed. She was sorry he wasn't there to read it along with her. So, she would take the three-hundred-fifty-six pages to Professor Hendricks in the morning, anxious to hear his opinion and suggestions on her work. Her fervent wish was that the finished product be worthy of the professor's memory.

George walked into the library where Samantha was working.

"Your young man is on the telephone. He is worried about you because you didn't answer your cell phone."

"Thanks, George, I guess I didn't hear my phone. If you're talking about Detective Fletcher, he's hardly my young man. He's probably calling with a question about the murder."

"Hello, Samantha, I'm sitting here with Robin and she insists you and I need a break from crime solving. Would you like to join me at Robin and Frank's house for chicken enchiladas? Frank is doing the cooking so we're safe from food poisoning."

Robin threw an eraser at his head and picked up the office extension.

"Don't listen to him, Samantha, I'm not a bad cook. I'm not a good one either, but I would never poison anyone. Anyway, we'd love to have you join us, that is if you can put up with our two rambunctious boys."

"I'd love it; thanks for asking."

Fletch spoke again, "I'm getting ready to leave the office; is it too soon to swing by to pick you up?"

"Not at all. I'll be ready when you get here."

George was looking on, smiling, not the least bit embarrassed that he'd been caught eavesdropping.

"The Professor would have approved of your young man."

"He's not my young man, George," Samantha said as the color rose in her cheeks.

Samantha liked Frank; he and Robin were perfect for each other. Their boys, Danny and Will, were the cutest little guys. It was truly a house filled with love.

Samantha was envious when Robin told her she was expecting another baby. She wondered if she would ever have a family of her own. Fletch watched her with the children and was having thoughts of the future as well. Whether he wanted to fall in love with this woman or not, he knew he was headed in that direction.

*****

While Frank and Fletch cleaned up the kitchen, Robin and Samantha sat in the family room. The boys were playing a game and were quiet for the first time that evening.

"Fletch is like a brother to me, maybe even closer than my own brother. He doesn't talk much about himself, but I know he was involved with someone who wasn't willing to accept his profession. It takes a special person to marry a cop. I think if, given a choice, Frank would prefer I was a nurse or a secretary, but he knows police work is in my blood."

"Is it that obvious I'm falling for the detective? I know how pathetic I must look in your eyes."

"You are far from pathetic. The man can't take his eyes off you. Even Frank noticed it and Frank is usually oblivious to that kind of thing. Fletch is a proud guy. He can't afford the lifestyle you are living and I think it intimidates him."

"He knows I'm not planning to stay at the mansion forever. The Professor asked me to find his daughter. He believed before he died that she was alive. I don't have any idea how to find her, but I feel I must try. I'd move out of there tomorrow if I didn't have the staff to worry about. Those people have lived there most of their lives. They would have no place to go without the mansion."

"I thought the professor left them all a generous inheritance."

"He did and they could all afford a place to live on their own, but they've become a family. I don't know what they would do without each other."

"Samantha, you're a good person; no wonder Fletch is crazy about you. I hope you can find the professor's daughter. I'll be glad to help in any way I can."

"Are you talking about Amari Stonehill?" Frank asked, as he and Fletch walked in from the kitchen.

"Yes, Professor Stonehill thought she was still alive. Frank, do you remember when she was kidnapped?"

"I think everyone who lived in Lancashire twenty years ago remembers that kidnapping. I was about twelve at the time and I was sure my baby sister would be the next victim. I slept with my baseball bat next to my bed for when the kidnapper broke into our house."

"I was the baby sister even though I wasn't a baby," replied Robin. "My brother used to torment me, telling me I was the next one on the kidnapper's list. He stopped after Dad heard him say it one time and grounded him for a month. It wasn't anything to joke about; everyone in town was scared to death."

"What was the feeling back then? Did people think the parents were covering up a crime?" asked Fletch.

"At first, everyone thought it was because the baby's family was rich. When there was no ransom demand, people began to talk. The Professor and his wife were both well-liked in the community but when tongues begin to wag, there was no stopping the rumors. Another theory that has stuck through the years is that the baby was sold. From all reports and the few pictures that were printed in the newspaper after her disappearance, she was going to be a real beauty. She was only two months old at the time, so it was hard to tell what she would look like in the future. It's now considered a cold case, Samantha, I don't know how far you will get. The Professor exhausted all avenues before giving up on finding her."

"We don't think he ever gave up. He might have had a private investigator working on the case when he died. What he uncovered could be the reason the professor was killed."

*****

On the drive back to the mansion, Fletch opened up to Samantha.

"It's nice to see a happy family, isn't it? The worst part of being a cop is being an eye-witness to family disputes. Before I was a detective, they were mainly simple squabbles that resulted from too much drinking in most cases. As a detective, too often the quarrel ends in death. I think Robin knows I need a break from the seedy side of life occasionally."

"Are you sorry you joined the force?"

"No, there are good times too. Like the time I arrested an innocent woman for murder and hauled her off to the station to interrogate her."

"You consider that a good time?"

"It turned out to be because I've grown very fond of that woman. I hope she has forgiven me and the feeling is mutual."

"She forgave you a long time ago and I suspect the feeling is very mutual."

Fletch pulled off the road to the shoulder.

"I've wanted to do this all evening."

He reached over and took Samantha in his arms. She readily responded to his kisses.

They could see lights shining as a car stopped behind them and then the lights began to flash.

Fletch rolled down his window and greeted the cop standing there with a surprised look on his face.

"Fletch, sorry buddy, I didn't know that was you. You might want to pull off the road a little further," the police officer said with a smirk.

"Stu, this is Samantha Degan; we're working on a case."

"I can see that; nice to meet you, Miss. Don't want to keep you from solving your case." He walked back to his patrol car, grinning.

"That was embarrassing, I haven't been caught making out in a car since I was in high school," said Samantha.

"Maybe we should take this back to my apartment where we won't be interrupted."

Samantha thought she should play hard to get but she didn't want to. "Wonderful idea," she said with a smile.

CHAPTER 18

"Bentley, I never see you anymore. Pamela is really keeping you busy," Gilford smirked as they were riding to the lawyer's office.

"I guess you could say that. Don't laugh, Gil; I think I might be in love."

"You in love, fat chance. You might be in love with her money but not with her. Get her to marry you, but after the honeymoon, we'll go back to being the Pennington brothers. We have a reputation to uphold."

"I don't want to live like that anymore, Gil. I want to marry Pamela and it's not only because her father's money will bail us out."

"Ben, what's happened to you? That girl has you brainwashed. Has she drugged you?"

"Don't be ridiculous. I'll be thirty years old on my next birthday and I haven't worked a day in my life. Pam's father has offered me a job and I'm going to take it."

"You've been reading those dumb letters from Mother again, haven't you?"

"Yes, I've read them all several times and it made me realize how worthless my life is. We could have done something to save Father's company, but we let some crooks take over and now there's nothing left of it. We're forced to sell the house our mother loved because we've squandered any money that was left to us."

"After our meeting with Edward today, we'll stop at Barney's. After a couple of drinks, you'll be able to think more clearly and forget this nonsense about a job."

"No, Gil, I'm not going to drink with you. In fact, Pamela has made me realize that I drink too much. I'm on the wagon now and I like being sober."

"You can't be serious. Who are you and what have you done with my brother?"

Bentley pulled the car into the parking lot of Edward Andersen's office.

"Here we are, ready to sign off on our childhood home. Let's get it over."

"We will continue this discussion when we're finished here. We'll have a nice check in our hands and that will make you reconsider about throwing your life away on domesticity."

"Don't waste your breath, Gil. I'm going to ask Pamela to marry me. I hope you'll be my best man, but if you don't think you're up to the job, I'll understand."

Gilford knew it was no use trying to change his brother's mind. He would go along with the marriage and pick up the pieces when Bentley came to his senses.

*****

Bentley spent a part of the proceeds from the sale of the Pennington mansion on an engagement ring for Pamela. She accepted his proposal and they were married two months later. Gilford acted as his brother's best man and behaved himself throughout the ceremony and the reception at the country club.

Mrs. Phoebe Winkler, widow of the late Edgar Randolph Winkler, was a guest at the wedding. She took a liking to Gilford and told her friends it had been over three months since her Eddy had passed on and it was time for her to move forward too.

Edgar had married Phoebe despite the forty-year difference in their ages. They'd only been married for two years when he died in his sleep. He often told friends that marrying Phoebe was the best thing he'd ever done and that he was sure he would live forever because she made him so happy. The doctors told Phoebe that Edgar's heart had given out from too much exertion.

Gilford moved in with Phoebe the day after his brother's wedding. Phoebe was the life of the party wherever they went. In many ways, they were well suited to each other and they settled comfortably into a relationship that was satisfying for them both. Gilford was sure Edgar's money would hold out for years and, unlike his brother, he would never have to work for a living.

In the meantime, Bentley and Pamela were happy in their lives together. Bentley found he enjoyed working and wondered why he had never tried it before this. He liked Phoebe and thought she brought out the best in Gilford.

Together and with the recommendation of counsel, the boys decided not to fight their Uncle Fenwick's will. "Let her turn it into an orphanage for all we care," said Gilford who didn't want to leave Phoebe while he returned to Lancashire for the court proceedings.

CHAPTER 19

"What are you two ladies giggling about?" asked Daphne when she saw Millie and Betsy standing in the hallway in front of Samantha's bedroom door.

"Miss Samantha didn't come home last night; her bed hasn't been slept in."

"That is none of your concern. Now get busy with your chores and stop your snooping."

Daphne knew exactly where Samantha had spent the previous night and she approved. Samantha had called Daphne the night before so she wouldn't cause her undue worry. *Samantha is the sweetest girl. If I had a daughter, I would hope she would be just like her,* Daphne thought to herself. *She and Detective Fletcher are a perfect match; it's a good sign that they are spending time together.*

*****

Samantha walked around the small apartment Fletch had brought her to last night. He was out getting breakfast for them at the deli around the corner. He ate very few meals at home and didn't have as much as a piece of bread for toast.

The apartment was sparsely furnished. Fletch had a sofa, a coffee table, a large television and a bookshelf in the living room. Samantha noticed a framed picture on the bookshelf along with several mystery novels by well-known authors. She picked up the picture. It appeared to be a photo of Fletch in a cap and gown. His family was circled around him. They were looking at him with such pride, especially his parents.

Fletch opened the door and the aroma of bacon from the breakfast he was carrying filled the air.

"That's my family if you hadn't guessed. I don't know why I keep that photo out; it was taken years ago. My brother and sisters were so young back then. The little one is in high school now."

"Do you miss your family?"

"Yes, I do sometimes, but my life is here now. I do get back home a couple of times a year."

Samantha put the photo back on the bookshelf and sat on the sofa to eat the breakfast Fletch had brought.

"I'm famished and this looks and smells so good."

"We worked up an appetite last night....and this morning."

Samantha could feel her cheeks redden. She wasn't the type to hop into bed after one kiss, but she had no regrets. She glanced at the photo again.

"What's so interesting about that picture, you keep staring at it?"

"It's not the picture itself. I just realized that I never did see a picture of the professor's wife on a table or shelf or anywhere in the mansion. There are photo albums in the library but they're of Bentley and Gilford and their parents through the years."

"Maybe he couldn't bear to have pictures of his wife around after she died. It might have caused him too much pain."

"That could be, but don't most people want to have something to remember their loved ones by. He talked about Veronica freely; I wonder why he didn't want to see her. I'll have to ask Daphne what happened to her pictures.

*****

After they finished their breakfast and got ready to leave the apartment, Fletch said he would like to hear what Daphne had to say about the lack of photos of Veronica Stonehill.

*****

"Welcome home, Samantha. I trust you had a good evening," Daphne said in a purely professional way. The servants all nodded to the couple without letting on that they knew where she'd spent the night. They didn't want to risk Daphne's wrath if there was even a hint of a knowing smile.

"Daphne, can you tell us why there isn't even one picture of Veronica or the baby in the house? Surely, the professor had photos of both."

"Yes, there was an album full of photographs of Miss Veronica and little Mari after she was born. I'm not sure where the album is. I assume the professor either destroyed it or locked it away somewhere. I haven't seen it since poor Miss Veronica died."

"Did he ever mention why he didn't have a photograph on any of his desks? Most men do have their wife's picture on their office desk, even if it was the wife who placed it there."

"I'm sorry, Detective, I don't know why. I do believe he did have Miss Veronica's picture on his desk in the library, but I don't know where it is now. I wish I could be more help. If you will excuse me, I should make sure Millie and Betsy are doing their chores properly."

"She's like a mother hen, isn't she?" Fletch said after she left the room.

"You must be right about the professor not wanting reminders of his wife around. He seems to have taken pains to remove all traces of her."

"I don't want to leave you, but I do need to get to the station. Will you have dinner with me tonight?"

"I'd love to but why don't you come here? We can have dinner in my suite. Have I told you about my bed?

It's very luxurious but way too big for only one person."

"I'm tempted to try it out now but duty calls and I'll have to wait until tonight."

Fletch gave her a kiss that held a promise of more to come when the door opened.

"I'm so sorry to interrupt you," said Daphne entering the room, "but I do remember there was a portrait of Miss Veronica right in this room above the fireplace mantle. The Professor had it taken down and replaced it with the landscape that's there now. I remember the framer told me the professor wanted the portrait discarded, but he couldn't get himself to destroy it and simply put the new painting over it. It must be under the landscape."

"I'll call George to bring a ladder to get that painting down. Maybe it's just curiosity, but I want to see what Veronica Stonehill looked like."

George came with a ladder shortly after Samantha called him.

"Miss Samantha, I'm sorry I didn't tell you sooner, but Calvin left for his hometown yesterday morning. His sister passed away."

"I'm sorry to hear that George. That must be Amy's mother. I'll have to send her a note. I hope you told Calvin to take as much time as he needs."

"I believe he's driving back to Lancashire as we speak. His sister had been ill for a long time. He mentioned there would be no funeral."

George was a large man. He stood on the ladder, lifting the painting off its hanger and easing it down into Fletch's waiting arms.

It was heavier than Fletch expected and he swayed when he caught it.

"That frame must be made of solid gold," he said.

Samantha grabbed the end of it and George helped once he was down off the ladder. They placed it carefully on the floor face down.

"Are you sure you want to do this, Samantha? I don't want to ruin the landscape."

"I'm sure. I know we should probably get an expert but we'll be careful not to tear the canvas."

George took his Swiss army knife and began to pull the staples out of the back. They slid out easily and the canvas popped out of the frame making it easier to manipulate. They all watched as George removed the last of the staples. He lifted the picture as the landscape lay on the floor. He turned it over and, indeed, there was the portrait of Veronica Stonehill.

Daphne let out a whimper as she looked at her former mistress.

"I'd forgotten how beautiful she was in those days."

Samantha's mouth flew open; she looked at Fletch and he had seen the resemblance too.

"It's Amy Brooks," she said.

"It does look like her," said Fletch. "She has the same coloring and the same smile; they could be twins."

"Or....mother and daughter. Is it possible Amy is Amari Stonehill?"

"What are you saying, Samantha?" asked Daphne. "That's impossible. Amy is Calvin's niece."

"Have you ever met Amy?"

"No, Calvin has never brought her or her mother to the mansion although the professor has told all of us that our families, if we have any, are welcome here."

"Maybe my imagination is getting the better of me. Do you remember where Calvin was the night Mari was kidnapped?"

"He was in the kitchen with us, wasn't he, George?"

"I'm not sure; he never stayed very long after we finished our evening meal. We always sat around the table and talked about the happenings of our day. Calvin usually excused himself and went back to his garage and his cars."

"What do you know about his sister? Do you remember him talking about the time his niece was born?"

"I remember," said Daphne, "it's a very sad story. His sister and her husband were expecting a baby. Calvin hadn't been working for the professor for very long, but he was always cheerful back then. He talked about becoming an uncle. He was excited about it and even thought about going back to his hometown to watch his niece or nephew grow up. I'll never forget the night he got a phone call from his mother. His sister and her husband had been in a terrible accident. His brother-in-law had been killed instantly and his sister was in a coma. The baby wasn't due for another couple of weeks but the accident caused his sister to give birth that very night. Calvin was beside himself. He loved his little sister with all his heart. He never talked much about his mother, but I got the feeling she was a difficult woman while she was alive. After the accident, Calvin didn't talk much. We'd ask him how his sister was doing and he'd say all right and that was it. We finally stopped asking.

"You have probably guessed that Calvin struggles a bit. I think he's had learning difficulties all his life. The Professor hired him out of pity, I believe, but he grew very fond of him."

"Are you saying Calvin kidnapped Amari and murdered the professor?" asked George. "I can't believe it."

There was a gasp and they all turned. Calvin was standing in the doorway.

"You're right, Samantha, I did those things," he sobbed. "I did it for my little sister, Ginny."

When the sobs subsided, Fletch told Calvin he shouldn't say any more without talking to a lawyer.

"Would you like me to arrange for a lawyer for you, Calvin?" Samantha asked.

"No ma'am, I want to get this off my chest. I have done terrible things and I need to be punished."

"Do you agree to let me record what you have to say, Calvin? You might be incriminating yourself if you continue to talk."

"I don't know what that word means but I do want to tell you what I did."

Fletch took out his phone and set it to record.

"This is Detective Joseph Fletcher of the Lancashire Police Department. I am at Stonehill Manor in Lancashire with Samantha Degan, Daphne Morgan, George Blake and Calvin Hensley.

"Calvin, do you understand I am recording the words you say and any information you give might be used against you in a court of law?"

"I understand, Detective Fletch. My sister died yesterday and there is no reason to keep the secret any longer. It's time Amy knows the truth.

Calvin told the story of his sister and her husband and the car accident that killed him and put her in a coma.

"Ginny's baby was born while she was in a coma. The doctors said she had a serious heart problem and she wouldn't live through the night.

"After two months of being unconscious, Ginny woke up. My mother had to break the news about her husband, but she couldn't tell her she'd lost her baby too. The doctors told my mother that Ginny had too many injuries and she wouldn't be able to have any more children.

"Mama told Ginny she was taking care of her baby girl and Ginny believed her. When it was time for her to leave the hospital, Mama panicked. She called me at the mansion and told me I had to find a baby for Ginny because she needed a reason to live. I told Mama I didn't know where I could get a baby and she told me there was a perfectly healthy baby at Stonehill Manor."

"But, Mama, that baby belongs to the professor and Miss Veronica."

"I thought you said they were gallivanting around out-of-town. They don't love that baby or they wouldn't leave her alone. Your sister will be a good mother."

"I can't do that, Mama; it's wrong."

"Calvin, it would be wrong to let your sister live her life without her daughter."

Calvin paused in his story and took a sip of the coffee Daphne had poured for him.

"Detective Fletch," he continued, "it was wrong of me to take Miss Mari from her crib. Mama said it would be all right but it wasn't.

*****

"Mama's house isn't too far from the airport. That night, I saw Miss Schindler leave to meet a man in the rose garden and that's when I went upstairs to the nursery and took the baby. I went down the back stairs and directly to the limo. I wrapped her in a blanket I had in the garage for cold nights. She was such a good baby; she never woke up. Everyone knew I was picking the professor and his wife up at the airport, so they didn't question why I was leaving.

"When I arrived at Mama's house, she had the nursery set up with everything a baby needs. I handed her Mari and left to drive the rest of the way to the airport.

"I felt sick to my stomach when Miss Veronica went on and on about how much she missed her baby and how she longed to hold her in her arms. I didn't know what to do; I couldn't let them know I had stolen their baby. I knew Mama and I would probably go to jail and then what would my sister do? She had nobody else in the world.

"My sister came home the day after I'd taken Mari from her crib. She was sad because her husband had died but she was crazy about her daughter. I couldn't take her joy away from her, so I said nothing.

"Mama told Ginny she needed a change of scene, she needed to start over in a new town. I think Mama wanted to get far away from home because she was afraid someone from the hospital would tell Ginny her real baby was dead.

Ginny never remarried; she lived her life for Amy. I think it broke her heart when Amy took a job at the Melbourne School, miles away from her home. About a year after Amy left, Ginny began to feel poorly. She thought it was a virus that would pass, but it turned out to be cancer. She had been sick for over a year before she passed away yesterday.

I went to see Amy at the school one time when I was running an errand for the professor. Her friend, Tim, took a picture of the two of us together. Amy gave me a copy of the picture. I don't remember Miss Veronica that well, but I do remember seeing that portrait of her. I knew if anyone saw Amy's picture, they would see the resemblance too. I liked looking at the picture because Amy was so pretty and so nice. One day, I was waiting in the limo for the professor. He didn't get out very much but sometimes had lunch with his friend, Professor Hendricks. I didn't hear them coming until they were almost to the limo and I jumped out of the car with the picture in my hand. I must have dropped it when I was helping the professor into the car. I saw it on the seat when I lifted him out after we got back to the mansion. He didn't mention the photo and I could only hope he hadn't seen it.

"Weeks went by and he didn't say anything about the picture. I had hidden it away in my dresser drawer and only took it out at night before I went to sleep.

"The Professor called me to his room that day. It was very early, but he said he needed my help. It was five o'clock and I was surprised the nurse wasn't there with him. He said she had to leave, but she'd given him a report that was delivered the night before. He didn't have to read it; I knew what it was going to say.

"Let me read this to you, Calvin."

"That's not necessary, sir, I think I know what it's going to say."

"I'm going to read it anyway. It's a report of an automobile accident involving your sister, Virginia Brooks and her husband Peter. You remember the accident, don't you, Calvin? Your brother-in-law died instantly and your sister was in a coma for two months. You do remember that she gave birth to a baby girl, don't you?"

"Yes, sir, I do remember."

"Do you also remember that the baby girl named Amy died when she was only hours old? It says here she had a serious heart condition. Did you know that, Calvin?"

"Yes, sir, I did."

"Your sister came out of her coma, didn't she, Calvin?"

"Yes, sir, she did."

"You were happy about that, weren't you, Calvin?"

"Yes, sir, very happy."

"The only problem was, she didn't have a baby anymore, isn't that true, Calvin?"

"Yes, sir, that's true; she didn't have a baby."

"So you decided to take my baby and give her to your sister, didn't you, Calvin?"

"Yes, sir, I took your baby."

"You are going to drive me to the Melbourne School where my daughter Mari is teaching and we will bring her home, isn't that right, Calvin?"

"I can't do that, sir; my sister is in bad shape. She has always believed Amy is her baby. If she finds out, it will kill her."

"I'm sorry about your sister, Calvin, but my wife died because of what you did. If you won't drive me to my daughter, I will call the police."

"He put the envelope with the report in the top drawer of his desk and reached for the telephone. I couldn't let him call the police; my sister needed Amy more than ever. I didn't want to hurt the professor, but I had to stop him. I picked up the letter opener on his desk and shoved it into his back. I grabbed the envelope and went back to my room and hid the report in my dresser along with Amy's picture.

"Don't you see? I couldn't let the professor take Amy away from Ginny. She didn't have anyone else."

Daphne's eyes were filled with tears.

"How could you do that to the professor and Miss Veronica?" she asked.

"I'm sorry, I'm so sorry. I never wanted to hurt the professor. I loved him. It seemed like the right thing to do at the time. I know I was very wrong. You can take me to prison now, Detective Fletch. It's what I deserve."

Calvin collapsed on the floor and curled into the fetal position. He was quietly sobbing.

Fletch turned his recorder off and called for an ambulance.

*****

The other servants came running when they heard the siren from the ambulance that pulled up in front of the mansion.

George scooted them back to make room for the paramedics to get through the door.

"Give them room to get to Calvin," he said. "There's no need to worry; they will help him."

"Why are Daphne and Miss Samantha crying? What has happened to Calvin?" asked Millie.

"Everything will be fine," said George. "All of you go to the parlor and wait for us. I will try to explain everything in a few minutes, not that I understand it myself."

*****

After stabilizing Calvin as best they could, the paramedics carted him off in the ambulance. The staff stood at the window in the parlor and watched as it disappeared down the winding driveway.

"Detective, how much of this can the staff be told?" George asked. "I should say something and I'd rather not lie to them."

"You don't have to lie, George. They will find out soon enough that the professor's daughter has been found and learn of Calvin's part in her kidnapping."

"Amy has to be told," said Samantha.

"Yes and as soon as possible," agreed Fletch. "She has been kept from her home long enough. Samantha, you and I are the only two people who know the story and have met her. Do you think you're up to talking to her about what transpired?"

"I really would like to tell her because the professor wanted me to find her. He must have seen the picture of Amy and Calvin and figured out Calvin was the one who took the baby from her crib. He probably hired the private detective to prove what he knew was the truth.

It's a sad story for everyone. Do you think Calvin thought he was doing the right thing at the time?"

"He thought he was doing the right thing for his sister, but I think he's had to live with his guilt all these years. The fact that he stayed here makes me wonder if he was punishing himself by having to see the torture Veronica and the professor were going through. I'm sure his mother knew just how to manipulate Calvin into doing the wrong thing for the right reason."

The staff and Samantha and Fletch all sat down in the kitchen to eat the meal that had been prepared before all the commotion. None of them were very hungry after what had transpired. Some were silent while the others asked questions that Fletch couldn't answer. Calvin was one of them and it was difficult for them to feel anything but pity for the man who was trying to save his sister from more suffering.

"As much as I'd like to try out your bed," Fletch whispered privately to Samantha, "I think I should let you get a good night's sleep tonight. I'll pick you up early tomorrow for our drive to talk with Amy."

"I'm not sure how much sleep I'll get tonight but that's probably a good idea. Amy just lost the woman she thought was her mother and now she will find out her whole life is a lie. I'm not looking forward to this visit."

Samantha slept fitfully that night. Her dreams were filled with crying babies being taken from their mother's arms. She woke up early and was waiting for Fletch when he arrived at the mansion.

CHAPTER 20

The sun was shining and the sky was a beautiful blue, the kind of day that made Samantha feel happy to be alive. Today, however, she hadn't noticed any of it. She and Fletch were on their way to meet with Amy Brooks. She had rehearsed what she would say over and over in her head all morning. How was she going to tell Amy that she had been taken from her mother so many years ago? She gathered from what Calvin had said that no one knew his secret except his mother who had died years ago.

"You'll find the words; I know you will, Samantha."

"You're reading my mind, aren't you? I pray you're right, I'm about to change Amy's life. Even her name is a lie."

"It will be a shock, but I think she's a pretty strong person. I'm glad you brought the portrait of her mother with you; she'll want to see what she looked like."

Samantha had rolled the portrait and brought it along with old photo albums of her father's. She looked for any pictures she could find in the professor's suite but had no luck. It would be nice if Amy could see photos of herself as a baby, especially if her mother was holding her in her arms.

They pulled into the long driveway. Samantha's heart was beating fast. Fletch noticed the color had drained from her face.

"I don't know if I can do this."

"Yes, you can; you know the professor would want his daughter to know who she is. I'll be right here beside you."

Amy greeted them at the door.

"It's so good to see you two again. As you can see, your gift of the van is being put to good use."

Samantha looked over toward the south entrance where she watched as several children were being loaded into the van.

"They are on their way to the zoo. Without your generosity, Samantha, trips like this would be impossible."

"I'm very sorry to hear about the death of your mother, Amy."

"Thank you. Although I'll miss her, she's free from pain now. How is Uncle Calvin today? He took Mom's death very hard."

"That's part of the reason we've come to talk to you. It's about Calvin and you."

"About us? I can't imagine what it would be; I don't know Calvin that well. I know it sounds strange but he always seemed to avoid me. I was surprised when he stopped by to see me a few months ago. He'd never been to the school before."

"Amy, I don't know where to start, what I have to tell you won't be easy for you to hear. I know you're close to Tim. Would you like him to be with you?"

"Tim's with some students now. Whatever you have to say can't be that bad. Is Calvin in trouble?"

"Yes, Calvin is in very big trouble. It started twenty years ago when he stole a baby from her crib. Amy, that baby was you."

Amy sat back in her chair. She simply stared at Samantha for what seemed an eternity.

"What is this all about? Who are you, Samantha, and what kind of scheme is this? Fletch, are you really a detective? I don't understand why you would go along with this nonsense."

"Amy," said Fletch, "hear Samantha out. I have Calvin's confession on tape. This is not a scam; I can assure you."

"All right, I'll listen to what you have to say, but my mother would never have allowed me to be taken by Calvin or anyone else."

"Amy, your name is Amari Joy Stonehill. You are the only daughter of Professor Fenwick and Veronica Stonehill. The man you thought was your uncle kidnapped you when you were two months old.

"I'm sure you were told of the accident that killed your father, Peter Brooks, and left his wife Virginia in a coma for several months. Ginny was pregnant at the time. The baby was born prematurely with significant health issues. She died shortly after her birth."

Amy lowered her head not knowing what to say. Samantha was telling the truth about the accident but the baby was her and she was very much alive.

"Your grandmother didn't think Ginny would be able to cope with the death of her husband *and* the loss of her daughter. She told Calvin the Stonehill baby was being neglected by her parents and Ginny would love the little girl more than they did. It wasn't true, of course, but Calvin believed you would be better off with his sister."

"That's impossible. How could Calvin have taken a baby from Stonehill Manor and not be found out? The Stonehills had more influence in this state than almost any other family. Surely, Professor Stonehill would have put the best detectives on the case."

"Calvin was never a suspect. It was thought he had left the estate to pick up the Stonehills from the airport when the kidnapping took place. As far as we can determine, he was never even questioned."

"My grandmother lived near the airport at that time. That doesn't mean he did this horrible thing. Why are you telling me now?"

"You are an extremely wealthy woman. The Professor, your father, never gave up on finding you. Calvin accidentally dropped a picture of himself and you standing in front of the school. The Professor saw the picture and recognized you because you are identical to his wife, your mother. He hired a private detective who verified that the baby born to Ginny Brooks died in the hospital."

"You say Professor Stonehill found the picture of Calvin and me, but the man is now dead."

"I don't want to shock you even more. Keep in mind, Calvin was trying to protect his sister. In his mind, he couldn't let the professor claim you as his daughter. He was afraid it would break Ginny's heart. I'm afraid he stopped him the only way he could think of at the time."

"In other words, he killed him. I do remember hearing about the murder. He was stabbed, wasn't he?"

"I'm afraid so, Amy."

"I still can't believe that I'm not Amy Brooks."

"I have a portrait of your mother if you would like to see it."

"Yes, I'd like that."

Samantha unrolled the canvas with the portrait of Veronica Stonehill on it just as Tim Griffin walked through the door.

"Amy, that's beautiful. When did you have it painted?"

Amy's eyes filled with tears. She knew instantly that the woman in the portrait was her mother. Everything Samantha had told her was the truth.

"Tim, that's not me; it's my mother."

Tim looked puzzled, "I never knew you were adopted. Not that it matters. I guess it never came up."

"I wasn't adopted. I was kidnapped and this is my real mother."

Tim sat beside Amy. He didn't say a word and simply rested his hand on her shoulder.

"Would you like to be alone, Amy?" asked Fletch.

"No, please stay. I have so many questions, I don't know where to start."

They all waited patiently while Amy regained her composure. She hadn't taken her eyes off the painting of her mother. Tim whispered to Fletch that Amy was his wife now. He told Fletch that they had been married in her mother's hospice room by a justice of the peace. It was Ginny Brooks' last wish that she could see her daughter married.

Finally, she asked, "Did my mother, I mean Ginny, know I wasn't her child?"

"According to Calvin, she never knew the truth. Your grandmother arranged for the family to move to another town where nobody knew them or knew about the family. Your grandmother kept Amy's birth certificate, but disposed of her death certificate."

"That means even my birth date is a lie. I don't remember my grandmother; she died when I was very young. The only relative I do remember is Calvin. One day we had a visit from an aunt. I think she was my father's sister. I can't even remember her name. I can remember Mom arguing with her. It surprised me because I'd never heard my mother argue with anyone before. I heard the woman ask her who my father was because I didn't look anything like Peter. I was only about seven or eight and had no idea what they were talking about. Several years later, I remembered the conversation and then I did understand its meaning. I never questioned my mother, but I did wonder why I didn't look like her or my father."

"Samantha and I will leave you alone. I know it's a lot to absorb at one time. We will be in town for the rest of the day if you need us for anything or have questions."

"Thanks, Fletch. I guess I do need some time for all of this to sink in. I think, in time, I will want to know more about my real parents. Now, I want to start the day over before I knew that Amy Brooks never existed."

Tim put his arm around her. "She'll be all right. I'm sure she'll be calling you later. If I know Amy, she will want to know everything about her other family."

*****

After Samantha and Fletch left, Amy sat at her desk and kept staring at the portrait of her mother.

"I feel like I'm in a dream and can't force myself to wake up."

Tim read a copy of the private investigator's report Fletch left with the couple.

"I can't imagine what you're feeling. This report rings true and because the woman in the portrait could be your double, I believe you are Amari Stonehill."

"Isn't it ironic that Amy and Amari sound alike? Two mothers who had no idea each other existed and yet they name their babies similar names. I don't know why that strikes me as odd. Nothing about this makes any sense to me. I feel loyalty to the woman I believed to be my mother and yet I can't ignore the fact that this stranger and I look so much alike. I never thought to ask if I had any siblings or any other relatives. You're right, Tim. I have so many questions for Fletch and Samantha. Would you call them for me? I think I'd like to go to Stonehill Manor. I want to see where my life began."

CHAPTER 21

Tim quickly arranged for other teachers to take his and Amy's classes for the next few days. After packing overnight bags, they met Samantha and Fletch at a coffee house in town.

"I think it's sinking in that I'm Amari Stonehill. That name is a mouthful, isn't it?" she smiled.

"Amari means *miracle*; they called you Mari. The Professor said you were a miracle baby because they didn't think they would be able to have children."

"I wondered if I had any siblings. I'm guessing I was the only one."

"You have two male cousins, Bentley and Gilford Pennington. They live in Pennsylvania. Their mother was your father's sister. She passed away recently. The Professor mentioned that an aunt and uncle raised your mother. I don't believe she had anyone else."

"This is such a shock to me that I forgot I attended a lecture given by Dr. Fenwick Stonehill once. I was in college at the time. It was one of the best lectures I've ever heard. I wanted to speak to him personally afterward, but so did most everyone in the lecture hall. Our bus was ready to leave for home and I couldn't wait."

"I wish you had been able to meet him; he was a fascinating man. I've called Daphne, who is the head of the household along with George, the general all around handyman. The two of them will be greeting you when we arrive. The other staff members will stay in the kitchen until you are ready to meet them. I know they will make a fuss over you but don't let them overwhelm you. They were all employed at the mansion when you were taken. The name Mari can't be mentioned without them tearing up."

"What in heaven's name am I going to do with a staff? I've never given orders in my life."

"You won't have to worry about that. If any orders are given, Daphne is the one to give them. She's a real sweetheart though and so is George."

"I know you said you were hired to write the professor's memoirs. I was just wondering...." She paused.

"You were wondering why I was still there."

"I'm sorry, Samantha. I didn't mean to pry."

"Don't be silly. That's a good question. Your father left Stonehill Manor to me in his will. He also left a note requesting me to find you. I have every intention of turning everything over to you, its rightful owner."

"I can't put you out on the street. I'm sure that's not what the professor would have wanted."

"Amy, I will be more than happy to relinquish my duties as mistress of the manor. As much fun as it's been to be pampered, I need to get back to reality."

"I'm not sure I'm suited to be mistress of the manor either," sighed Amy.

*****

Fletch and Tim made the two-hour drive in separate cars. Amy jotted down questions she had for Samantha on the way. She thought they would never get there and became more anxious as every mile brought them closer to Stonehill Manor.

Tim followed Fletch down the winding road to the mansion. Amy's eyes were as big as saucers.

"I knew they called this a mansion, but I had no idea how huge it is. Oh, Tim, I think we should turn around and go back home."

"Let's check it out. Remember Samantha's idea of turning it into a school. We would be able to help even more children here. Look to the left, there are stables and I see horses in the meadow."

He parked behind Fletch and they all got out of the cars. Daphne and George were standing at the door.

George had to steady Daphne when she saw Amy. Tears were streaming down her cheeks.

"Miss Mari, you are finally home and you are so beautiful. You look exactly like your mother."

George was having a difficult time keeping his composure.

"I believe she prefers to be called by the name Amy," he said. "Don't let the girl stand out here while you blubber."

Amy told the elderly couple how pleased she was to meet them and introduced Tim. She walked through the doorway and into the massive foyer. Her eyes widened as she glanced around the room. She felt Tim clasping her hand as the realization of her enormous wealth began to sink in.

"Would you like a tour? We'll go through the house first and then to the kitchen where I'm sure the rest of the staff is waiting impatiently to meet you," said Samantha.

Amy and Tim were speechless as they walked hand in hand through the hallways and into the rooms. As Samantha planned, their last stop was the kitchen where there wasn't a dry eye gazing at Amy. She greeted each one individually and asked their names and what their jobs were.

"Are you going to sell our home, Miss Mari... I mean, Miss Amy?" asked Millie.

"Don't be impertinent, Millie," cautioned Daphne.

"That's okay, Daphne, they have a right to know what my plans for this place are. Although the reality of my identity hasn't had a chance to sink in, Samantha has told me how important Stonehill Manor is to all of you. I grew up in a three-bedroom ranch home on less than a quarter-acre of land. I can't picture Tim and me living here by ourselves. That doesn't mean you will be displaced. Samantha has given us an idea and if it's possible, we would like Stonehill Manor to become a branch of the Melbourne School."

"Calvin told us about your school, Miss Amy. Children who can't walk live there, don't they?" asked Betsy.

"Some are unable to walk on their own, some have other physical limitations but they are all eager to learn. We have several children who live at the school. We also have those who live in their own homes and attend the school during the day. If the plan works out, we will need the services you provided for the professor. I'm afraid the children will keep you much busier than you have been in a very long time."

"We would like that, wouldn't we, everybody?" said Gretchen, and the others nodded their heads in agreement.

"Tim and I will be going back to our home now, but we will be back to work out the legalities and make plans for remodeling the mansion. Thanks to all of you for making me feel so welcome. Samantha has agreed to stay on until we can figure out all the details."

After Amy and Tim left, the group was abuzz with excitement. They were looking forward to a houseful of children they could make a fuss over.

CHAPTER 22

Three months later.

Renovations were underway at the mansion. Tim and Amy had settled into her father's suite. In time, that room would be remodeled but it was important that the children's dorm rooms and classrooms be finished before the beginning of a new semester.

What had been several guest bedrooms were divided into four spacious sleeping areas for the younger children and two areas for the older children, giving them their own spaces but being certain they had the companionship of each other.

Additional elevators had been installed in each wing and classrooms would soon be equipped with the latest electronic devices.

Shortly after Amy discovered her identity, she met with the professor's lawyer and was given a report on the extent of her newly acquired wealth.

"Tim, I don't know what we will do with all that money. The school has scrimped and saved for so many years and now it is set for a lifetime. As soon as we are finished with the renovations at Stonehill Manor, we will remodel and update the Melbourne School too. We can hire more teachers and buy all new equipment for the classrooms."

*****

One afternoon, while the noise of construction was dying down for the day, Daphne opened the front door of the mansion.

"Mr. Bentley, what a surprise. Was Miss Samantha expecting you this afternoon?"

"No, Daphne. After the way I behaved, I was afraid Samantha wouldn't let me anywhere near this place and my cousin, Mari."

Daphne reluctantly opened the door for him and his young lady to pass.

"I'll call Miss Samantha and Miss Amy—that's what Miss Mari prefers to be called." Daphne found it difficult to hide her true feelings of Mr. Bentley Pennington as she left the room to fetch her mistresses.

"She doesn't like you very much, does she, Ben?"

"No, Pamela. I told you I had some fences to mend."

Samantha and Amy walked to the parlor where Bentley and Pamela waited.

"Bentley, how nice to see you." Samantha was forcing a smile. "This is your cousin Amy Griffin; Amy meet Bentley Pennington."

"Amy, it's wonderful to meet you. My brother Gilford and I were very happy to hear the news that you were found. May I present my wife, Pamela?"

"It's nice to meet you too. You must excuse our mess; we are in the middle of making renovations. Stonehill Manor will be a school in another month or so. I hope you aren't here to object to the plan."

"No, not at all. I think it's a wonderful idea. As a matter of fact, if Gil and I hadn't been forced to sell the old Pennington mansion, I think it would have been nice to make it into something useful too. These old mansions are luxuries from the past."

Samantha couldn't hide the surprised look on her face. Was this the same Bentley Pennington who drank the professor's liquor supply dry?

"I think I'd better get to the point of my visit. Of course, I'm happy to meet my cousin but there is another reason, one I'm not proud of."

Pamela reached out and took his hand encouraging him to continue.

"As Samantha knows, Gilford and I came to Stonehill Manor after our uncle's passing to take what we could get from what remained of his estate. Uncle Fenwick, your father, was a very astute man. He knew the kind of lifestyle my brother and I preferred and wisely left the bulk of the family legacy to Samantha. He trusted someone he'd known for a matter of months over his own nephews. We were furious and resentful of the woman who we thought had schemed to steal our rightful inheritance.

"In the time we were here, we realized there was nothing we could do to change our uncle's will. We remembered from playing here as children, that there was a safe in Uncle Fen's suite. In our distorted sense of entitlement, we found that safe again and were able to open it. This metal box was in the safe. Gil opened it and found these."

Bentley opened the box to show an array of sparkling jewelry.

Samantha and Amy let out gasps.

"There must be thousands of dollars' worth of jewelry in there," said Amy.

"That's what we thought until we took it to a pawn shop and were lucky to have escaped with our lives. You see, this jewelry is all fake. It's not unusual for the owners of expensive jewelry to have copies made and hide the real pieces away in a safe-deposit box in a bank. We assume that is what Uncle Fen did. I believe the key to that safe-deposit box is in the safe. Gil remembers seeing it but didn't make the connection at the time."

"Tell them what else you found in the safe, Ben," said Pamela.

"I also found a bundle of letters my mother had written to Uncle Fenwick through the years. She worried about Gilford's and my behavior. She asked him for help with us in every letter. I never realized the grief we had caused Mother until I read her words. I never saw Uncle Fen's replies to her but I can only surmise he told her she had spoiled us beyond redemption and there was nothing he could do to change the pattern."

"He was wrong," said Pamela. "Bentley did change his ways thanks to those letters."

"Yes, thanks to the letters and to the love of a wonderful woman, I am a changed man. Pamela and I knew each other years ago, but she came back into my life shortly after I left Stonehill Manor. You won't believe this Samantha, but I am a working man. I'm working in Pam's father's company."

"He's very good at it too. Daddy's company is too important to him not to hire the best," Pamela said with obvious pride.

"I'm so happy for you, Ben," said Samantha. "You look happy and healthy. Has Gilford mended his ways too?"

"He's a one-woman man now. He and the widow, Phoebe Winkler, are busy spending her late husband, Edgar's, hard-earned money. I think the two of them are on an African safari this month. It's difficult to keep track of where in the world they are at any given moment. They are well-suited for each other, but I don't know what they'll do if and when the money runs out. I don't see much of my brother anymore. He thinks I lead a boring life."

Amy was looking through the jewelry. "The girls would have such fun playing with this stuff; they love bling and she held one of the flashier pieces to her neck. She then picked up another smaller piece with a single gem in the center. This is the necklace my mother was wearing in the portrait; I think I'll hold on to this one."

"There's a portrait of your mother? I don't remember seeing any kind of pictures here. That's why I took the time to look through the photo album in the safe. I had forgotten what Aunt Veronica looked like. Amy, you look very much like her."

"Did you say there was a photo album in the safe?"

"Yes and a couple of stacks of photographs. I didn't see them all because Gil was anxious to get out of there before we were caught."

"Ben, I would love to see those photos. Can you tell me where the safe is? Tim and I are living in those quarters now and I don't remember seeing a safe."

"Sure, it's behind a picture on the wall and it's not easy to spot. I think Gil found it when we were young because he was always snooping for secret panels in this old place. I'll show you exactly where it is. The combination is my mother's birthday, so I should be able to open it."

They all ran up the stairs to the third floor to Amy's suite. Ben walked directly to a painting on the wall and felt around the edges until he unlatched it from its false frame exposing a large wall safe. He unlocked it on the first try and stood back while Amy reached in. She pulled out the photo album and slowly opened it. There were pictures of her mother alone and with her father. Page after page of places they'd been together. As she neared the end of the book, there were also pictures of them holding a baby. The others looked on silently as Amy's eyes filled with tears. She saw herself as a smiling, happy baby being held in her mother's arms as she looked adoringly at her child.

"We should leave you alone, Amy," said Pamela.

"No, please stay. I will have plenty of time to cry over these photographs. I'd like to see what else is in here."

She reached in and found a large envelope. It contained her parent's marriage license and her birth certificate along with several other legal documents. She found the key to the safe-deposit box where it was assumed the priceless jewelry would be found. She asked Pamela if there was anything she would like from the collection, otherwise, she would give it to a museum. She had no use for fancy jewelry but she would keep the one necklace her mother seemed to wear in most of the photos. There were over ten years of journals her mother had written. After she read them, she would discover that the single stone necklace had been a gift from the professor the day he was told he would be a father.

Bentley and Pamela left Stonehill Manor with the promise the cousins would keep in touch. Pamela had some ideas for decorating the children's bedrooms and would bring some sketches on her next visit.

Between the photographs and her mother's journals, Amy began to feel real ties to the Stonehill family. She would always love the woman she thought was her mother, but her heart was opening to the woman who gave birth to her. She wondered if she had always somehow felt her presence in her life even before she learned of her existence.

Epilogue

Six months after renovations began, the Stonehill Manor School was ready for the new school term.

A gala was being held at the school to introduce it to the people of Lancashire and the surrounding area, and in celebration of the publication of Professor Stonehill's memoirs. There was already talk of a movie being made of his life. Samantha's writing career was off to a grand start.

Bentley and Pamela were in attendance along with Gilford and Phoebe. Samantha was happy that both Pennington brothers had found happiness in their own way. Pamela whispered to Amy and Samantha that a new little Pennington was on the way. Amy was looking forward to the day when she would be making the same announcement.

Samantha moved out of the mansion and into her own apartment. She had to admit she would miss the staff and especially Daphne and George. It had been an interesting experience. She was surprised and happy to find that Amy had arranged for her big comfortable bed to be delivered to her new apartment.

Fletch asked her to move in with him but he understood she needed to go slow in their relationship. They fought their feelings for each other for a long time and Samantha needed time to trust that those feelings were genuine.

*****

The party was in full swing when the Mayor of Lancashire arrived. Fletch had known the Honorable

Robert Delaney since his first days on the force. He introduced him to Samantha.

"Samantha Degan, it is a pleasure to meet you. I have just finished reading Professor Stonehill's memoirs and I don't believe you could have portrayed him any better. The entire city is proud of that man."

Samantha couldn't help but notice Fletch was slightly uncomfortable with the conversation. He walked away to get them another drink from the bar and when he returned, Samantha told him the Mayor had invited them to join him for a musical his wife was starring in at the community theater.

"Samantha, it's my job to be cordial to our illustrious Mayor, but I don't want to spend an evening with him. He's a known ladies' man and I don't want you falling for his malarkey."

"Joseph Fletcher, I do believe you are jealous," she laughed.

"I'm just telling you to be cautious."

"I'm sure he isn't going to be seducing me in front of his wife; she's standing over there."

"That's not his wife."

"Oh, well, I'm afraid I committed us to seeing his wife, whoever she is, in a show tomorrow night. Are you upset?"

"No, but I can guarantee your seat will be next to the Honorable Mayor of Lancashire."

*****

The next evening, Samantha and Fletch met the Mayor and his entourage in the lobby of the local theater. He handed them both tickets. They took their seats and

Fletch winked at Samantha when she was seated next to Mayor Delaney.

At the end of the second act of the musical, when the band was playing its loudest and the entire cast was marching down the aisles to the tune of "Seventy-Six Trombones," Samantha felt the Mayor's head on her shoulder. She sat straight up and his head fell into her lap. She was frozen in her seat before she tapped Fletch on his arm.

Fletch could see the blood beginning to ooze from the mayor's mouth. He felt for a pulse.

"The Mayor is dead, Samantha."

THE END

ABOUT THE AUTHOR

 Jane O'Brien is a wife, mother of three, and grandmother of five. Jane and her husband, Dave, have lived in several states in their over fifty years of marriage. They are retired and live in Northern Colorado. Jane enjoys writing mysteries and family and friendship novels. *Murder in Stonehill Manor* is the first in the Samantha Degan Mystery series.

Follow Samantha Degan and Detective Joseph Fletcher as they investigate the death of His Honor Mayor Robert Delaney in the mystery coming soon— **Murder in Lancashire.**

www.ingramcontent.com/pod-product-compliance
Lightning Source LLC
Chambersburg PA
CBHW020340260626
47156CB00004B/1622

* 9 7 8 1 9 4 6 0 6 3 1 6 8 *